UNDERTAKER'S FRIEND

ROGUE LAWMAN NINE

PETER BRANDVOLD

WOLFPACK
PUBLISHING
— EST 2013 —

Undertaker's Friend
Print Edition
© Copyright 2022 (As Revised) Peter Brandvold

Wolfpack Publishing
5130 S. Fort Apache Rd. 215-380
Las Vegas, NV 89148

wolfpackpublishing.com

Paperback ISBN 978-1-63977-211-7

UNDERTAKER'S FRIEND

GIDEON HAWK FOUND A SHELTERED PLACE TO CAMP for the night along a pristine mountain lake. From a high ridge, the lake had resembled a heart-shaped nugget of ornamental turquoise shimmering against the gauzy green velvet of a fir and spruce forest.

Hawk stripped tack from his grullo mustang, rubbed the horse down thoroughly and carefully with a swatch of burlap, then picket-pinned the stalwart, loyal, but nameless animal in the trees at the edge of the camp.

The bivouac sat on a ledge maybe thirty feet above the lake. The ground was spongy and layered with pine needles and other forest duff. The cool air owned the heady tang of pine resin. Tall evergreens protected the campsite on the side sloping down from the ridge. On the north side was the lake over which a cool, refreshing breeze whispered.

No trouble was likely to come from the lake. If

trouble came from the ridge, the grullo would give a warning.

Hawk gathered wood and built a small fire. He made sure his Henry repeater was loaded and leaning nearby. He brewed a pot of coffee on an iron tripod mounted over the stone fire ring he'd built to contain the flames, and sat back against the woolen underside of his saddle to smoke a cigarette and to enjoy the piping hot brew as well as his view of the lake.

As the sun angled down in the west, tree shadows stretched long and dark across the water. The breeze died. The water turned to glass.

Hawk lifted one knee, leaned back on an elbow, and looked around. A rare serenity settled over the rogue lawman, though the perpetually grave set of his face did not betray this fact. He was alone here. He might have been the last man. All was quiet. A bald eagle dropped low over the lake until the curved talons hit the water with a splash.

The raptor rose skyward on its heavy wings, a writhing, silvery fish trapped in its feet. It gave a shrill cry of satisfaction as it caromed off toward a darkening northern ridge where it would dine on its fish.

The only sounds were the breeze playing in the crowns of the pines up near the top of the southern ridge, and, nearer, the pleasant snapping and crackling of Hawk's small fire. The smoke smelled good. Occasionally, when a vagrant breeze turned the smoke toward him, it burned his eyes and peppered his coffee with gray ashes. But even that was pleasant here on this lonely promontory over an isolated mountain lake, at the end of another hard-fought blood trail.

Hawk sipped his coffee. Staring out over the lake, he sat up straighter and narrowed his jade-green eyes, which shone in sharp contrast to his dark skin tone and the severe facial features he'd inherited from his Ute war chief father. The eyes were the same color as his Norwegian immigrant mother's.

Hawk's heartbeat quickened slightly.

He wasn't alone, after all.

On the far side of the lake, someone had walked out of the trees and was striding purposefully toward the shore, which dropped gradually to the darkening water. The figure, tall and slender, appeared from this distance to own the curves of a woman. The fading light flashed salmon on the white blouse and touched the long, auburn hair gathered into a tail, which was pulled forward to hang over her right shoulder.

Hawk grabbed his field glasses and adjusted the focus.

A woman, all right. Fairly young, judging by how fluidly, lightly she moved. How straight and plumb the line of her body was, the breasts firm and pointed behind the blouse. She wore a long, dark skirt and dark boots.

Where in the hell had she come from?

She walked down the slope to the edge of the water, where she paused, staring into the lake.

That side of the lake was maybe seventy-five yards from Hawk. In the sphere of his magnified vision, he saw the grave, pensive expression on the young woman's oval-shaped, even-featured face. She'd likely be pretty if he saw her close up. She stood there for a time, not looking around, not seeming to enjoy the scenery of the place, but only staring at the water.

A strange apprehension touched Hawk.

"What're you thinkin' about...?"

It was as though his throatily uttered muttering had prompted her to action. She stepped forward into the water. She kept walking straight ahead, as though she thought she was walking on dry land. The water quickly moved up past her ankles to her knees, the soaked skirt clinging to her legs.

The water rose from her knees to her thighs... and higher... to her waist.

Still, she kept walking until the water was up to her breasts. Then her head slipped under and she was gone.

Hawk lowered the glasses, scowling, narrowing his eyes. He raised the glasses again. All he could see of the woman were the ripples ringing out from the place on the water where she'd disappeared.

Hawk fiddled with the focus wheel, as though that would somehow bring her head back to the surface.

"What in tarnation...?" he grumbled, lowering the glasses once more.

His heart thudded.

He set the glasses down, rose quickly, and, casting anxious glances at the far side of the lake, kicked out of his boots and peeled off his socks. Working hastily, muttering to himself, he shrugged out of his cracked leather, wool-lined vest and chambray shirt and skinned out of his black whipcord trousers and long-handles. Naked, he ran to the edge of his camp, leaped onto a flat rock overlooking the water, and dove forward off the balls of his feet, lifting his arms straight up above his head.

He drew a deep breath as his large, muscular body arced through the chill air, and then the lake wrapped itself around him, feeling warm until he reached the nadir of his plunge. Then the icy mountain chill bit him deeply. He arced back to the surface, lifting his head, quickly getting his bearings, and started swimming quickly but fluidly toward the lake's far side, keeping his head above the surface.

When he thought he was near the place where the woman had disappeared, he drew his knees toward his chest and flung his arms and head forward and down. He swam toward the bottom, reaching ahead and pulling the water back behind him.

The water was as clear as polished glass, so he saw her right away—a slightly blurred figure floating below him and to his right. She appeared to be kneeling in the water roughly two feet above the lake's sandy bed, as though she were giving praise. Her hair and blouse and skirt billowed around her. Her arms floated upward. As Hawk swam to her, he saw that her eyes were closed and that she wore a serene expression. Air bubbles rose from her nose and slightly parted lips.

Hawk grabbed her around her waist and pulled her to the surface. He thrust his head out of the lake and drew a deep breath, shaking water from his face. He slid his left arm up beneath her shoulders, lifting the woman's head out of the water, as well, and then began swimming toward the nearest shore, the one she'd come from.

Letting her head rest against his shoulder, he dragged her through the water as he swam awkwardly, using one arm. His feet scraped the lake's shelving bottom. He stopped swimming and trudged up the steep shelf, grunting with the effort of pulling the woman along, the level of the lake dropping down his chest to his knees and finally to his ankles.

He picked the woman up in his arms. She was much heavier now than she'd been in the water, the lake streaming off her sodden body and her hair, which hung now like a single, soaked, brown rag. As Hawk carried her onto the shore, he looked down to see that she still wore the same serene expression as before.

Hawk laid her on the grass several feet up from the gravel and sand. He stared down at her, puzzled. He placed a hand on her belly. She didn't appear to be breathing. He'd never tried to save anyone from drowning before. He drew a deep breath, thought it through.

He had to get the water out of her lungs.

He reached down and began to press on her belly, then, reconsidering, turned her over so that she lay belly down against the grass, and placed his hands on her back. He leaned forward, putting a good bit of his own weight on her body.

Nothing.

He pressed again, released the pressure, then leaned against her, pushing hard on the middle of her back. He did this several times, putting more and more weight on her, imagining her lungs expanding and contracting, until she convulsed and made a gurgling sound.

Her face was turned to the side. Her eyelids fluttered. Her mouth opened. Water gushed out of it onto the grass.

Hawk pressed down hard on her back again.

Again, she convulsed.

When no more water issued from between her lips, which appeared thin and blue, Hawk turned her over onto her back. The serene expression was gone. Now deep lines scored her pale forehead, and her lips were stretched back from her teeth. Her eyelids fluttered. She writhed on the ground, shaking her head.

"No," she moaned. "No, no."

She shivered, lips quivering, teeth clacking.

Hawk looked around. The sun was almost down. The lake had turned nearly black. Only a little green light remained in the sky.

He glanced back over his shoulder to stare across the lake. He could see the flickering orange flames of his cookfire on the stony ledge on the lake's far side, gray smoke unfurling skyward. Imagining the caress of those warm flames against his cold, soaked body made him shudder with anticipation.

He had to get himself and the girl—she was somewhere between a girl and a woman, he thought—to the fire.

Hawk rose, pulled his charge up by one arm, crouched, and settled her onto his right shoulder. As she continued to choke and cough, convulsing on his shoulder, occasionally mumbling, "No, no," he began walking along the shoreline, following the curve toward the far side and the gray smudge of his stony bivouac.

Hawk looked around cautiously, making sure that he and the girl were alone out here. He was naked and unarmed. Being a hunted man, such a state was deeply uncomfortable.

It was nearly dark by the time he gained the base of the ledge on which he'd camped. He had to look around for a time to find a way up into the outcropping. Finding a long, narrow, steeply meandering cavity, he shifted the girl onto his other shoulder and began climbing. By the time he'd reached his camp, he'd scraped his bare feet raw and bloody. His fire had burned down to feebly glowing coals.

He lay the girl down beside the fire, on his own spread soogan, by his saddle and saddlebags. She was shivering and groaning, writhing and muttering. Hawk set some crumbled pinecones on the fire, and blew on the coals. When small flames began licking against the tinder, he slowly added slivers of dry firewood. The flames grew, crackling, snapping, and smoking.

Hawk, shivering, turned to the trembling woman.

"Gotta get you out o' them duds," he grumbled.

She stared up at him now, but he wasn't sure she saw him. She seemed only half conscious, maybe in shock.

He unbuttoned her blouse, then slid it off her shoulders. She did not resist but only stared up at him, shivering. He lifted her camisole and chemise over her head, and tossed them onto the rocks to dry by the fire. The pale globes of her breasts sank against her chest, perfectly round and full, the pink nipples jutting. He removed her boots, wool stockings, and then her skirt. He was going to leave her drawers on, but when she began fumbling with them, trying to peel them down her thighs, he helped her.

He tossed the drawers onto the rocks.

He looked down at her lying before him, naked. She had a beautiful body—full-busted, flat-bellied, round-hipped, and long-legged. Her lips were beginning to get some fullness and color back. Her eyes were lilac blue.

Hawk knelt between her spread legs. He stared down at her. Her eyes held his.

The warmth of the fire pushed against him, and he stopped shivering. He became aware of the desire warming his nether regions, and he glanced down to see that he was fully erect. She lifted her arms and opened her hands, reaching for him, staring at him, parting her lips.

Her breasts were rising and falling heavily, her belly contracting and expanding sharply as her breathing quickened.

She closed her hand over his jutting shaft. At first, her hand was cold. He flinched. Quickly her hand warmed, warming him. His heart thudded.

She kept her gaze on his. Her eyes were slightly crossed. She canted her head slightly to one side and made a grunting sound of desperate desire, hardening her jaws.

Hawk lowered himself over her. She spread her legs farther apart, grunting and raising her knees. Hawk lowered his head to hers, mashed his mouth against hers, and slid into her warm, wet opening.

CHAPTER 2

HAWK HADN'T MADE LOVE WITH SUCH RAW POWER and passion in a long, long time. The woman seemed to devour him. She writhed beneath him, bucking against him, moaning. Anyone watching would have thought, wrongly, that she was fighting him.

At the apex of their coupling, she gave a long, guttural groan and clung to him as though he was all that was holding her back from a fall into a dark abyss. Finally, long after they'd stopped shuddering together, she released him. Her body relaxed against the ground.

Hawk rose and, warm now from exertion, gathered his clothes and dressed. She sat up and, raising her knees to her breasts, watched him. Her wet hair, littered with dirt and pine needles, clung to her shoulders. She looked like some wild woman of the forest.

Hawk said nothing as he built up the fire.

Still, she watched him, saying nothing. She arranged her clothes on rocks nearer the fire, to quicken the drying, and then sat on the ground again, a blanket wrapped around her shoulders. She watched Hawk in hushed silence as he set about putting another pot of coffee to boil on the tripod.

When the coffee was done brewing, he poured two cups and handed one to her.

Behind him, the grullo whinnied.

Hawk spun, his .44 Russian instantly in his right hand, the hammer clicked back. The flickering fire-light shone in two eyes staring at him from the forest. Two horse eyes. The horse's ears twitched, curious.

"It's all right," the woman said, her voice husky and hoarse behind Hawk. "He's mine."

Hawk turned back to her. She looked at the silver-chased revolver in his hand. Hawk depressed the hammer, dropped the popper back into its holster positioned for the cross-draw on his left hip, and snapped the keeper thong in place over the hammer.

Hawk sat on a rock, picked up his coffee, and studied her through the wafting steam. He didn't know what to make of her. Something told him she would entertain no questions. That was all right. She likely wouldn't ask any, either. That, too, was fine with him. He didn't much like talking about himself. In fact, he didn't like to talk much at all about *anything*.

He didn't know why she'd tried to drown herself, and it wasn't his business to know. People had their reasons. They didn't always feel the need to share those reasons with others.

It hadn't been Hawk's place to save her. He'd done so automatically, without thinking about it. Maybe he hadn't been sure she'd wanted to die. Now, having saved her and made love to her—if you could call what had happened here around the fire anything close to love—he knew that's exactly what she'd attempted to do. She'd wanted to die.

Maybe she'd try it again. It was no business of his. If he chose a similar course of action, which wasn't out of the question, he wouldn't consider it anyone else's business. In fact, he felt a little guilty now for intervening. He didn't usually trifle in other people's business as long as they didn't trifle in his.

Hawk drank half of his coffee, then reached into a saddlebag pouch for a small burlap sack of jerky. He placed a couple of pieces in his left hand, drew the top closed, and handed the sack across the fire to the woman.

She shook her head, sipping her coffee.

Hawk set the sack down, then leaned back against his saddle. He drank his coffee and ate the jerky. He built up the fire again and then set to work cleaning and oiling his guns. He could feel her eyes on him, watching. By the time he was finished with that chore, she rose, removed the blanket from around her shoulders, gathered her clothes, which appeared nearly dry, and started dressing.

She didn't look one bit shy about dressing in front of him. Why should she, after what they'd done? Still, some women would.

When she was finished, she threw her hair, which was also nearly dry but still dirty, out from the collar of her blouse, and said, "I'll be going."

Hawk frowned as he slipped his Colt into its holster. "Dark out there."

She jerked her chin toward the southeast. "Moon on the rise. Small one, but I know the trail."

She walked over to her horse, which was saddled, and toed a stirrup. She swung up into the saddle.

"Here," Hawk said, taking the blanket to her, holding it up to her. "It's a cold night. You'll need this." She didn't have a jacket, and he knew her clothes were still damp.

She took the blanket, wrapped it around her shoulders, and dipped her chin. It was an acknowledging nod. She looked at Hawk. It was as though she wanted to say something but couldn't find the words. He gazed back at her, waiting.

She sucked her cheeks in, then reined her horse around, touched heels to its flanks, and rode away. The hoof thuds dwindled gradually.

Hawk was sitting by his fire, sipping another cup of coffee, when he heard the thuds of her horse's hooves again on the far side of the lake. She'd ridden around to the side he'd first seen her on, and was retracing her route to wherever she'd come from.

The night was so quiet, the air so still and dense, that he heard her horse kick a stone. The stone rolled briefly, clattering. The hooves continued to thud for a time, the sounds dwindling again gradually, until there was only the silence of the night weighing down around the solitary man by the fire.

Hawk finished his coffee. The fire burned down to glowing embers.

He rolled up in his soogan, tipped his hat over his eyes, and slept.

———

Arliss Coates rode her gelding, Frank, out of the forest and onto a shaggy, two-track wagon trail touched with blue light shed by the kiting quarter-moon. She stopped the horse and looked both ways along the trail.

Which direction was town?

Getting her bearings by the moon's position, Arliss reined Frank to the left and began heading northwest along the trail. As she heeled the horse into a trot, however, she began to feel an invisible hand pushing her away from the town of Cedar Bend.

She did not want to return there. Or, more specifically, she did not want to return to the house she shared with her husband, Roy. But there was nowhere else for her to go.

Or was there?

She gave a shudder as she imagined the lake's dark chill. Of walking into it again, at this time of night, of taking a deep breath of water to push the life out of her, and reclining on the sandy bottom forever.

Again, she shuddered. The mountain night air was cold, and her clothes were still damp. They smelled of the lake she remembered walking into as though it had been a dream she'd dreamt several weeks ago.

Had she really done that? Tried to *drown herself*?

When she'd ridden out of Cedar Bend that afternoon, she'd had no intention of doing anything like what she'd ended up doing. She'd merely felt the walls of that house—of *Roy's* house—closing in on her, with its baskets of Roy's laundry to wash and dry and iron and Roy's meals to cook, and his wood to split because he'd been grazed by a bullet a couple of months ago when he'd been trying to stop a fight between two drunks in Miss Pearl's Red Light Parlor, and he claimed it still bothered him.

But, of course, any work bothered Roy. Arliss had found that out not two days after they'd been married and Arliss had moved into the house he'd built when he'd become town marshal of Cedar Bend. He'd built the house for himself and his then-wife, Charmian, who'd died during a stagecoach robbery two years ago. Ten years Arliss's senior, Marshal Roy Coates had seemed so strong and capable. A strong, noble man. Maybe a little stern, but, like her father had told her, good men were stern. Weak men were soft.

Well, Roy had turned out to be both stern of temperament and soft of character... at least when it came to doing anything except coming home from work and sitting in his rocking chair and drinking whiskey or ale and lamenting the death of his beloved Charmian.

Of course, Arliss didn't know for sure that lamenting his dead wife was what he was doing, but she'd once caught him studying a tintype of Charmian with a look of longing in his eyes. Arliss suspected that Charmian had been Roy's first love, and losing her had been the heartbreak of his life. He'd married Arliss because she was young and pretty, and she was the daughter of a wealthy man.

But he hadn't loved her. In fact, Arliss got the very real sense that her presence in Coates's house was almost an affront to Roy's memory of Charmian. Arliss only reminded Roy of who *wasn't* there. Arliss was an imposter. After the first few months of marriage and his initial delight in her young, supple body, Roy had turned away from Arliss. He'd started to resent her. She'd seen it in his eyes, which hardly every looked upon her anymore, and when they did, it certainly wasn't with anything akin to fondness.

When he was drunk, which he was nearly every night, he often regarded her with a toxic mixture of lust and shame. Never with love.

So those walls had been closing in on Arliss Coates, formerly Arliss Stanley, who'd grown up on her family's Circle S Ranch in the mountains and was accustomed to some space around her. She'd never been a stranger to work, but somehow working for Coates was far different from working around the ranch with her mother and her brother, Johnny. That work had been fun. There'd been camaraderie in it, and there'd always been a hired man around to flirt with and to make Arliss feel young and alive and desirable.

Now, there was nothing but Coates's laundry and his cooking and his firewood to split and his garden to tend—a garden that Charmian had likely tended so much better—and the incessant ticking of the wooden wall clock that had been an heirloom of Charmian's family.

So the walls had been closing in... and Arliss had saddled Frank for a ride in the mountains, and the next thing she knew, she'd been walking into the chill waters of Pine Lake. Her family had once picnicked on Sunday afternoons around the lake when Arliss was a little girl. Her father had taken Arliss and Johnny hunting near the lake, as well.

She supposed walking into those cold waters had been her way of going back in time, of returning home when she had no other home to return to. She was no longer welcome at the ranch.

Again, she gave an involuntary shudder, thinking how much colder and darker those waters were now, so many hours after the sun had set... imagining herself lolling in the lake's frigid depths.

She recalled the man who'd pulled her up out of those depths. She remembered the heavy, rugged weight of his body atop hers, the sweet pain of his hardness inside her, sliding in and out of her, making her feel young and alive and desirable again, just as she had in what now seemed so many years before...

Arliss reined Frank to a halt on a low dike, and stared down the rise's far side and into the night-cloaked valley in which Cedar Bend lay. Again, she felt that invisible hand pressing against her chest, holding her back from the town. Revulsion for Coates's house, Coates's life, was a heavy brick in her belly.

She must have ridden for close to an hour after leaving the dark, green-eyed stranger on the ledge above the lake. She'd been so deep in thought as Frank had negotiated his own remembered way out of the mountains that it seemed like only a few minutes had elapsed since the stranger had reached up to give her the blanket that was still wrapped around her shoulders.

It smelled of him.

Earthy and musky with man sweat and old leather, and a faint touch of juniper, maybe cedar...

She found herself turning her head to stare up into the dark mountains blotting out the stars behind her. Her breasts tingled as she remembered his hands kneading them, his mustached lips suckling them. Warm blood of remembered desire pooled in her lower regions.

She shook her head, turning forward to gaze out over her horse's raised ears. The warmth of chagrin crept into her cheeks.

My god—what a harlot she'd been. Toiling like a she-bitch in heat with some aimless drifter, possibly an outlaw, judging by all the guns he carried and how well he carried them. Yes, an outlaw. He was probably holing up in the mountains, on the run from the law. Arliss doubted she'd ever see him again, which was as it should be.

Still, the thought gave her a vague but bitter disappointment as she booted Frank down off the rise and headed along the trail toward the flickering lamplit windows of Cedar Bend and the only home she had.

CHAPTER 3

ARLISS FOUND HERSELF SO DEEP IN THOUGHT AGAIN that instead of circling around the outskirts of the town, she rode right through the heart of Cedar Bend via the town's broad main artery. Right past the town marshal's office, where Roy likely was—unless he was "patrolling" one of the parlor houses, as Arliss was well aware he tended to do.

She knew he frequented such places because she herself had seen him coming and going from Miss Pearl's or another house called the Alley Cat on the town's rough-hewn southern end, when she'd been strolling around the town's backstreets on nights she'd found herself feeling especially homesick and claustrophobic and unable to sleep or focus on needlework.

At first, she'd been hurt and angry that her husband was being unfaithful to her. Not so recently, however, she'd become glad Roy visited those places. It meant he'd come calling on his wife for such pleasures less frequently, though Arliss suspected that it wasn't so much pleasure he sought from her. What he really wanted was to punish her for being there in his house, taking the place of Charmian. His lovemaking had been pleasant for maybe the first few times. Forever after, it had been most unpleasant, indeed—more angry and violent than passionate.

Fortunately, he didn't force himself on her more than once every two or three weeks these days.

Arliss gritted her teeth as she watched the marshal's office slide past on her right. It was a low, L-shaped, mud-brick building with bars over the windows, and a wooden front veranda. A sprawling cottonwood abutted its right end, offering shade on sunny summer days. A lamp lit the two front windows, but Roy usually left a light on, even when he wasn't in the office.

He was likely out on "patrol," which was just fine with Arliss. She released a held breath of relief as Frank trotted on past the place, but then she gritted her teeth again when hinges gave a dry squawk from the direction of Roy's office.

"Arliss?" Roy's voice.

Oh shit, oh shit, Arliss thought.

She kept her head forward and continued riding, the blanket billowing out in the night air around her, like wings.

"Arliss, is that you—where you been? I been lookin' all over for you!"

She glanced over her shoulder as she continued

putting distance between them. "Just went for a ride, Roy. Heading home!"

"Arliss!" Roy shouted. She cringed at the exasperation in his voice.

On her left, men's laughter sounded. Arliss glanced over to see three or four townsmen standing outside the Arkansas River Saloon, a couple with their hips hiked on a porch rail. They held drinks and cigarettes or cigars in their hands. They laughed with subtle mockery as they switched their gazes from Roy to Arliss, then back again.

"Arliss, goddamnit, get back here!" Roy bellowed. She could really hear his anger and frustration now. It caused his voice to gain that brittle shrillness she knew so well.

"I'm chilled, Roy," Arliss called behind her again. "I'll be at home!"

She rammed her boot heels into Frank's flanks, and the horse broke into a gallop.

Louder laughter erupted behind her.

A minute later she rode up to the stable flanking Roy's house on a barren lot at the northeast edge of Cedar Bend. Having been raised on a ranch, she knew that tending her horse took precedence over her own needs. When Frank had been rubbed down, fed, watered, and led into the small corral that abutted Roy's stable, Arliss drew the stranger's blanket more tightly around her shoulders and strode from the stable past the single-hole privy and a small, dead tree to the house's rear door.

She grabbed an armload of wood from the pile by

the door and let herself inside the house. She shivered in delight at the thought of a hot bath. She carried the wood up through the short hall and was surprised to see the glow of a lantern on the other side of the flowered curtain that partitioned the hallway off from the kitchen and small parlor.

Tentatively, Arliss slid the curtain aside. Her stomach dropped when she saw Roy sitting at the end of the kitchen table over which the hurricane lamp hung, sputtering slightly, smoking.

"Roy," she said in surprise.

He sat casually in the chair, one arm hooked over the back. One boot was hiked on a knee. Roy was an austere-looking man, thirty-two, with wavy, dark-red hair and a thin mustache. His gray eyes were set too far to either side of the bridge of his wedge-like nose, which was a little flat and knobby due to its having been broken and not set correctly.

His forehead was broad, high, and lightly freckled behind an unnatural pallor somewhere between cream and tan. He wore a red bandanna wound tightly and knotted around his thick neck, at the open collar of his powder-blue work shirt.

A five-pointed star was pinned to the shirt's breast pocket. A Remington revolver was holstered on Roy's right thigh.

He rested one thick hand on the table, the fingers slightly curled inward.

His eyes were hard as he studied her. Through them she could see the roil of anger inside him.

"I didn't expect you home so soon," Arliss said, faking a smile and trying to sound casual.

"Come here."

"What?"

"Come over here. Stand in front of me. Let me get a look at you."

Arliss hesitated, then swallowed. Slowly, she walked around the table to stand before her husband. Again, she smiled.

"Sorry if I worried you. I didn't mean to be gone so long." For some reason, she had found herself keeping up the pretense that they were a happily married couple—that she loved him, that he loved her. She wasn't sure why. Maybe because the truth seemed so harsh and raw and terrifyingly lonely that she didn't really want to believe it deep down, though she did.

"Where've you been, Arliss?"

"I told you. I went for a ride in the mountains. I got turned around. When I finally realized I was heading in the wrong direction, the sun was nearly down." She chuckled, though it sounded phony and wooden even to her own ears.

"You grew up in those mountains. You couldn't get lost up there."

"I guess I got distracted."

Roy reached up and felt the arm of her blouse. It was a quick, brusque movement with absolutely no tenderness at all. He could have been cleaning his fingers on the fabric.

"You're blouse is damp." He grabbed her skirt, rubbing it between his fingers. "The skirt, too."

"Frank spooked and pitched me into a creek." Arliss chuckled again, her heart thudding apprehensively. "I'm fine."

"Frank, huh?" Roy sneered. "I never did trust that horse. Has a look in his eye. Too much stable grain. What he needs is a good, hard quirtin'. Don't you worry..." He rose from his chair and started toward the curtained doorway.

"What're you doing?" Arliss asked.

Roy stopped. "I'm gonna quirt that horse long and hard. He needs some of that contrary taken out of his hide."

"Don't you dare!"

Roy looked incredulous. "*What*?"

"Frank is my horse, remember? My father gave him to me for a wedding present. He's *my* horse—not yours. And no one will ever lay a hand on him!"

"He needs a good, hard quirting, I tell you, Arliss. He's gotta learn to respect..."

"Or maybe I... *I* gotta learn." Arliss's heart was beating fiercely. Rage burned her ears. It was all coming out now—all the pent-up anger and frustration. It was like opening a window in a shut-up room, letting the stink out. "Isn't that right, Roy? Maybe it's I, your wife, who has to learn some respect? Isn't that what you really mean?"

Roy turned full around to her, glaring down at her, his own rage burning like a flame in his distant eyes. "Why did you back-talk me out there on First Street, for all to hear?"

"Is that what this is about?"

"Those men—good friends of mine... they were laughin' at me. Laughin' about the way you talked *back* to me!"

"I see," Arliss said, crossing her arms on her breasts, smiling without humor. "Now I see what this is about."

Roy curled his upper lip and turned back to the curtained doorway. "That horse needs a good quirtin', all right. And I'm just the man to give it to—"

"Stop, Roy!" Roy always kept an old Remington revolver hanging from a peg in a square-hewn ceiling support post by the range. Arliss grabbed the gun now and, holding it in both hands, aimed it at her husband. She hardened her jaws and narrowed her eyes. "If you go anywhere near my horse, I will blow your head off, Roy!"

Again, Roy turned full around to her. Fury bleached his face, drawing down his mouth corners. His right cheek twitched. He walked toward her, his nostrils expanding and contracting, his broad chest rising and falling sharply.

"You put that gun down."

Arliss ratcheted back the hammer. "You stay away from Frank."

"I'll do whatever I think is right. Now, put that gun down. I won't tell you again!"

"Stop!"

Roy kept coming, taking one slow step at a time. His mustached lips stretched a challenging grimace. "Go ahead," he said. "Pull the trigger. I dare ya."

Arliss wanted to. Oh, god—how she wanted to!

She'd never known how badly she wanted to shoot him, probably *had* wanted to since the second month after they were married, when she saw him leaving Miss Pearl's with a sheepish grin on his face and she realized that their marriage was a sham.

As Roy kept moving toward her, she tried to squeeze the trigger. But her finger seemed frozen in place, merely resting against the trigger. She bit her lip, but she couldn't fire the gun.

Roy jerked his arm up and sideways, against her hand holding the gun. The gun discharged with an angry *crack*. The bullet tore into the ceiling, causing dust to sift onto the table. The gun flew over the table to bounce off the front wall and clatter onto the floor.

"Bastard!" Arliss screamed.

Roy backhanded her hard. She twisted around and flew forward against the table. She tried to push off the table but Roy pressed himself up against her backside, pinning her there. He sniffed her neck and then the blanket hanging off her left shoulder.

"What's that smell?" Roy sniffed the blanket again, like a dog. "What is that?" There was a stretched pause. He lifted the blanket to his face, scowling down at it, giving it a good, long sniff. "That ain't no smell I recognize. That's a *man's* smell."

"Roy, let me go!" Arliss screamed, trying to push him away from her.

He held her fast against the table, pinning her arms to her sides. "Who's that smell, Arliss? Who does that smell belong to?"

"Roy, no!"

"Who?"

"Roy!"

"That's why you're wet—ain't ya? You tried to wash his smell off. But you didn't do it." Roy sniffed the blanket again, then tossed it away. "You tried, but you couldn't wash his smell off, Arliss. Who was it? You tell me, you hear? I'm gonna ride up into them mountains, and I'm gonna kill the son of a bitch!"

"Roy, you're crazy! Let me go!"

"You think so, do you? You think I'm just gonna forget that you rode up into them mountains and rutted like a back-alley cur with some man? Ha!" Roy started to slide her skirt up her legs. "You lie beneath me like I'm somethin' you're just toleratin', waitin' for it to be over. But you go up into them mountains and you rut like somethin' *wild*! Ain't that right, Arliss?"

"Stop!" she screamed.

"No, I ain't gonna stop!"

He continued to slide her skirt up her legs. She could feel his heart beating fiercely against her back. She could also feel his desire. His body was hot, fairly trembling with lust. Imagining her with another man had aroused him!

"Oh, god—stop, Roy!"

He slammed her face down against the table. Keeping her pinned to the table with his body and with one forearm pressed against the back of her neck, he reached up and pulled down her pantaloons and drawers. He was breathing hard, grunting and sighing. Arliss tried to lift her head but there was no give in Roy's arm nor in his body rammed against her.

He ripped the pantaloons off her with a loud, grating grunt, and flung them away. He did the same to her drawers.

"Roy... Roy, goddamn you," she sobbed, feeling him moving around behind her, bending his knees, unbuttoning his pants. "Roy, stop," she said, her voice trembling, tears trickling down her cheeks. "Stop this, right now, Roy! I'll tell my father!"

"You do that," Roy said, and then she could feel his engorged manhood pressing against her as he spread her legs apart with his right knee. "You do that, and you also tell him about the man you fucked in the mountains!"

Arliss gave a grating cry against the tearing burn as he rammed himself into her, his arm pressing even harder against the back of his neck.

Mercifully, he finished quickly.

He pulled away from her with a grunt and stumbled backwards, his breath rasping in and out of his lungs. Arliss was too weak to stand. There was a horrendous burning in her belly. She dropped down the end of the table and collapsed onto the floor.

She lay on her side. She snaked one arm across her belly and drew her bare legs up. Roy stood over her. He was still breathing hard, shoulders rising and falling heavily. He glared down at her, stretching his lips back from his teeth.

"Now, that we've come to an understandin'," he said, his voice phlegmy, "I reckon I'll get back to work."

He grabbed his Stetson off a hook by the door, and left.

Arliss drew her knees to her belly, gritting her teeth against the pain of the vicious attack, against her rage and hopelessness.

She closed her eyes and cried.

CHAPTER 4

THE NEXT DAY, LATE MORNING, HAWK HALTED HIS grullo on a rise and found himself staring across a broad valley toward a town sprawled across a chunk of dun-colored prairie about one-mile square.

He hadn't known there was a town out here. But, then, he'd never been to this neck of the frontier before. That was why he was here now. Since he lived to kill those who deserved killing, he tended to cut broad swaths and burn bridges. He figured few people would recognize him here. With this neck of the territory being fairly well off the beaten path, he likely wouldn't be hunted here by those who were hunting him, either—namely, deputy U.S. marshals and bounty hunters, the occasional Pinkerton.

While Hawk hadn't known there was a town out here, he'd figured there must be one around somewhere. When he'd left his bivouac earlier that morning, he'd come across a trail that had appeared well traveled, scored as it was by both horse and wagon prints. It had appeared a well-maintained stagecoach run.

Most well-used trails, especially stagecoach trails, eventually led to towns.

He was gazing across a valley at such a town now.

An instinctive apprehension touched him. He usually avoided towns. For such a man as Hawk, towns often meant trouble. But since he'd never visited this one before, the chances of trouble catching up to him here were slim.

Also, he didn't intend to let any grass grow under his feet in the town beyond. He was low on trail supplies. He'd stop in town long enough to fill a couple of croaker sacks with possibles, including a few bottles of whiskey, and then he'd ride south and west. His intention was to wend his way back to a cabin he maintained in the remote San Juans. He'd hole up there for a month or two while his back trail cooled and then, before the autumn cold and snows came to the high country, he'd ride south to spend the winter in Arizona or northern Mexico.

Surely, he'd find some men who needed killing in Arizona or Mexico. Most likely, both places. Everywhere on the frontier were men who needed killing. Even some women. Hell, Hawk couldn't think of a place on god's green earth that wouldn't be better off with its human herd culled. That's how he saw himself —a culler of the human herd.

He looked down at the badge he wore pinned to his shirt, partly covered by the left flap of his wool-lined leather vest. It was a deputy U.S. marshal's badge that he usually wore upside down, for that's also how he saw himself—as an upside-down lawman. There was no need to advertise himself here, however. He unpinned the badge and shoved it into a pocket of his vest, where it snuggled with the small horse his late son, Jubal, had carved from a chunk of oak.

The horse and an ambrotype photograph of Jubal and his dearly departed mother, Hawk's beloved wife, Linda, was all that Hawk had to remind him of his family so brutally taken some years ago now by "Three Fingers" Ned Meade.

Hawk brushed his hand across the Russian revolver positioned for the cross-draw on his left hip, then lifted his reins and clucked to his horse, which started down the rise. Fifteen minutes later, he walked the horse along the main street of the town, which a badly weathered sign jutting up from a clump of rocks and buck brush at the town's outskirts had identified as Cedar Bend.

A fairly typically rough-hewn ranching supply town, Hawk thought. A dozen or so wood frame or adobe brick false-fronted building establishments, some a combination of both, some shaded by a cotton-wood or two. Nothing made the settlement stand out from any of the other such places he'd visited on his travels across the frontier.

Hawk angled the grullo toward one of the three hitchracks fronting the Arkansas River Saloon. He had few weaknesses, but a drink in a quiet saloon now and then was one of them. He'd have that drink, possibly two or three drinks, then stock up on trail supplies in the mercantile he'd spied another block to the south, then head back to the mountains long before sunset.

Now and then he'd imbibe in the pleasures of a whore, if he could find one to his liking. One that wasn't liable to leave him with a burning case of the Cupid's itch. That was another weakness of Hawk's. The occasional need for a woman. He wished it wasn't, but he was a man with a man's desires, and there it was.

Fortunately, his carnal sojourn of the evening before with the pretty young woman he'd saved from the lake had satisfied that need for the time being. Hawk wondered about her in a vague sort of way. He didn't like to get sidetracked by abstractions, and ever since she'd ridden out of his camp, that's what she was. An abstraction.

Hawk tied the grullo to the hitchrack, mounted the veranda, and pushed through the batwings. The place was pleasantly quiet. It smelled of sawdust and beer. There were only five other customers drinking at various tables in the long, narrow room, and two business types in bowler hats standing facing each other at the bar, sudsy mugs of brown ale in their fists.

They all looked at Hawk, raising their brows with interest. The wanted circulars his face adorned notwithstanding, such wistful gazes were to be expected. Hawk knew he cut a singular figure. Not only was he tall, dark, and green-eyed, he also wore two big, well-kept pistols. Obviously, he was no traveling minstrel.

When Hawk was satisfied none of the men around

him were bounty hunters or federal lawmen or Pinkertons, he walked straight ahead to the bar at the back of the room. A snarling bear's head was mounted above it and so were several sets of deer and elk antlers. A dapper little man, bald-headed and wearing armbands on the sleeves of his ruffled shirt, stood behind the bar, gazing at the newcomer through wide, light-blue eyes.

The eyes had a childlike quality. They were filled with awe now at the impressive-looking stranger standing before them. The mustache of a proud lion mantled the small barman's upper lip. It must have been the little man's way of compensating for his diminutive, otherwise nondescript stature.

"Help you, stranger?" the little man asked in a little man's feminine voice, giving one sweep of his mustache an absent tug.

"I'd like a bottle of whiskey. Not one you brew in a stock trough out back, but somethin' you got with a label on it. I'm gonna take it over there and drink down part of it, and if I like it, I'll take two more."

"Oh," said the little man, as though he found the order somewhat peculiar and maybe a little fascinating. "Well, all right, then." He turned to look up at the shelves of his back bar, lifting a delicate hand and brushing his tapering fingers across the labels. "Well, then... let's see. How 'bout this one here? It comes up from Texas. A little spendy, but if it's good tangleleg you're lookin' for, then this is probably the best one I sell."

"You recommend it?" Hawk said.

"Uh, well... yes," said the little man, flushing a little as he ran his pale-blue gaze across his customer's broad shoulders. "But, uh... with reservations... and a nod to individual taste, of course. If you don't like that one, I'll buy you a taste of somethin' else. How would that be?"

He suddenly seemed a little worried the newcomer might get colicky and start shooting up the place.

"All right," Hawk said, typically taciturn. "How much?"

"Let's just see if you like what you drink out of the bottle, and then we'll settle up," said the little man, holding up his delicate hands in supplication.

"All right," Hawk said, picking up the bottle in one hand and grabbing a shot glass off a near pyramid with the other. "Obliged."

He started to turn away. The little man said somewhat sheepishly but affably, "Where... where you from, stranger?"

Hawk glanced back at him, brows ridged.

The little man slid his eyes to the two others standing to Hawk's right. They both looked down. The little barman moved his pale, thin lips inside his mustache, as if to speak, but no sounds came out.

Then he just held up one of his pale hands again in supplication, waving off the ill-advised query and smiling.

Hawk took his bottle and glass over to a table at the side of the room, about halfway between the front wall and the bar, kicked out a chair, and sank into it. He kept his back to the wall.

He glanced at the other customers. They were watching him furtively. When his eyes met theirs, they turned away quickly and resumed the conversations they'd been involved in when Hawk had walked in and they'd found themselves distracted by the curious newcomer.

Hawk popped the cork on the bottle and filled his shot glass. He sipped the whiskey, rolled it around in his mouth, let it wash to the back of his tongue, and swallowed. He looked at the barman. The little man was watching him expectantly. Hawk pooched out his lips and dipped his chin with approval.

The barman smiled and gave an end of his outlandish mustache a tug.

Hawk finished off the first shot of the whiskey. Already, the forty-rod was warming him, sanding off the sharp edges. The saloon was cool and dark. He liked the molasses-like tang of drink that permeated the air. He liked the hushed murmur of the conversations. He liked the crude but homey way the place was outfitted. He even found himself liking the little barman with his preposterous mustache, who was now running a rag over the top of the bar and conversing with the two businessmen drinking before him.

Hawk kicked out a chair to his left, and crossed his boots on top of it. He refilled his glass and sank back into his chair, enjoying himself. He sipped the whiskey slowly. It wasn't the best he'd tasted, but he'd tasted worse. It would do for these parts.

He'd drunk down half of his second shot when the drum of galloping hooves rose in the street fronting the place. The men around him stopped talking and, frowning, turned to stare through the dusty front windows. Hawk squinted against the outside glare. Three horseback riders galloped past the place, a couple of pedestrians hurrying to keep from being trampled. When the riders had disappeared to the north, their dust hung heavy in the air behind them.

The other men in the saloon muttered darkly, one grimacing and shaking his head. One said, "That's what happens when you spare the rod."

"Ain't that a fact?" said the man he shared a table with.

Hawk finished off the second shot and refilled his glass. He liked it here. He'd stay another twenty minutes or so, then head over to the mercantile. Besides, his horse needed a rest before it climbed back into the mountains.

Hawk raised his shot glass to his lips but pulled it down when two men walked quickly past one of the two front windows. They wore dusters similar to those of the three who'd galloped past the saloon. They were moving too quickly for Hawk to get a good look at them, but he thought both wore neckerchiefs up over their faces. A second later they pushed through the batwings, guns raised. They had their faces covered, all right.

"Everybody just sit still and there's a *chance* you won't get hurt!" said the one wearing a red neckerchief with white polka dots drawn up over his mouth and nose. A curl of thick blond hair hung down over his right eye.

"Oh, shit!" said one of the customers sitting directly across the room from Hawk.

"Oh, shit, is right!" said the second man who'd entered the saloon with his gun drawn. He laughed, grinning behind his green bandanna. He was shorter than the first man but broader through the waist and shoulders.

A door flanking the bar opened, and a third man entered the room wearing a bandanna over his face. This man was more fashionably dressed than the other two. He seemed to fancy himself a gunfighter, for he wore a low-slung holster thonged on his thigh. The holster was trimmed with three hammered silver *conchos*.

Conchos also decorated the leather belt around his waist, below his cartridge belt. He wore Mexican *charro* slacks with the traditional flared cuffs, and a light-blue shirt embroidered with fancy red stitching tracing the outlines of two curvy, naked girls. His crisp tan Stetson had a snakeskin band.

"This here's a holdup, Mister Pevney," the third man said, proudly, waving his silver-chased Colt pistol around. He pulled a burlap sack out from behind his cartridge belt, and tossed it onto the bar. "Kindly fill that sack for me, please, and don't be holdin' out on me. I know you did a whoppin' business last night, it bein' payday out to the Crosshatch, and every Crosshatch rider spendin' the whole long night in town!"

The dapper little barman glowered red-faced at the holdup man who fancied himself a border tough. "Johnny Stanley, who are you tryin' to fool with that neckerchief up over your face? Don't you think I know it's you?"

He thrust a hand over the top of the bar, pointing out the other two hardtails also waving their pistols around. "And that's Avril Donnan and Dave Yonkers. You boys put away them guns and get the hell out of here before I send for Coates!"

"Can't fool an old fool, I reckon, boys!" Chuckling, the would-be border tough jerked his bandanna down off his face. He aimed his pistol toward the bar, narrowing one eye and clicking back the hammer.

The little barman gave a yelp and pulled his head down as Johnny Stanley blasted a forty-four round into the back bar mirror. The mirror shattered, the glass raining onto the floor.

The little barman lifted his head and turned to his mirror in horror. "Good god! *You got any idea what that mirror cost me?*"

Stanley aimed his pistol at the little barman. "The next one's gonna be drilled right between your beady little eyes, Mister Pevney... less'n you get to fillin' that bag right quick." He turned to slide his gaze across the other customers, including Hawk. "The rest of you start diggin' your valuables out of your pockets and layin' 'em out on your table. My pals Avril and Dave will walk by to collect momentarily, and if all goes well, and none of you hoopleheads piss-burns me too bad, we'll be on our way. If I even *think* any of you upstandin' citizens of Cedar Bend is holdin' out on me, I'm drill you a third eye. Understand?"

The little barman grabbed the burlap sack off the

bar and, looking constipated, took it over to where he apparently kept his cashbox under the bar. The others in the room began emptying their pockets onto the table. Avril and Dave began making the rounds, holding their own bags open so the customers could drop coins and bills and wallets and timepieces into them.

The toughnut who Pevney had called Dave—the stockier of the first two men who'd entered the saloon —walked over to Hawk's table. He'd removed his neckerchief from over his face, as had Avril. Dave scowled at Hawk, who was staring at Dave over the rim of his half-raised shot glass.

Hawk's boots were still crossed on the chair.

"Hey, you—what makes you think you're so special? Empty them pockets. Lay it all out on the table, now, you hear?" Dave aimed his cocked Schofield at Hawk's face.

CHAPTER 5

HAWK STARED AT DAVE OVER THE RIM OF HIS SHOT
glass, which he was turning very slowly in his fingers.

Dave looked aghast, frustrated. He turned to
Johnny Stanley, who was just then accepting the burlap
sack back from the little barman. "Hey, Johnny—this
son of a bitch 'pears to be wantin' for that third eye
you was talkin' about."

Johnny cradled the bag in his left arm and looked
at Hawk. "Oh, yeah?"

Sneering, he walked over to stand beside Dave,
scowling down at Hawk.

"What?" Johnny said. "You think you're too good
to get robbed, Mister?"

Hawk sipped his drink and then set it on the table.
"No. And you three ain't too good to get dead."

"What's that supposed to mean?" Dave asked.
"Can't you see we both got our guns aimed at you, you
cork-headed fool? Who are you, anyways, and what
makes you think you can talk to us like that? We're

here to rob you, and that's just exactly what we're gonna do. You ain't no better than these other hoopleheads."

He glanced at the barkeep and the other customers.

"You'd best think it through," Hawk said, staring up at Johnny through those cold, green eyes.

Johnny's scowl deepened. His dimpled cheeks flushed, and his eyes blazed with anger. "No, you'd best think it through, you simple fool!" He wagged his Colt at Hawk. "You get your valuables up here on the table or I'm gonna blow your head off!"

Hawk stared back at Johnny for a full five seconds. Then he turned to Dave, also scowling at him but looking a little skeptical, fearful. His cocked Schofield was shaking slightly in his hand.

Hawk cast his glance over Johnny's left shoulder, toward the bar, and lifted his right cheek with a shrewd grin. Johnny and Dave both did exactly what Hawk knew they'd do. Believing someone was making a play behind them, they cast quick, cautious glances toward the bar.

Hawk gave his table a violent shove with both hands, ramming it into both Johnny and Dave. The two would-be saloon-robbing desperadoes were pushed backward, off-balance.

As they yelled and swung their pistols back toward Hawk, the rogue lawman drew his Russian with his right hand and his Colt with his left hand.

The Russian roared a wink before the Colt, knocking Johnny backward. Screaming, Johnny trig-

gered his own Colt into the ceiling while Dave drilled
a round into the very edge of Hawk's table.

Rising from his chair, Hawk calmly clicked the
hammers of both his pistols back. He aimed at Johnny,
still stumbling backward, raking his spurs along the
floor. Hawk's Russian punched a round into Johnny's
right shoulder, evoking another shrill, girlish scream.

Meanwhile, Dave was reestablishing his balance
after tripping over a chair. Just as he got his Schofield
leveled on Hawk again, Hawk's Colt roared, drilling a
round into the dead center of Dave's chest. Dave triggered his Schofield into the wall behind the rogue
lawman, then threw his arms up as though he was
surrendering. Then he dropped straight back onto the
table behind him, jerking and flopping his arms and
legs as he died.

The third toughnut, Avril Donnan, stood on the
other side of the room from Hawk. He was dancing
around, yelling, trying to get a clear shot at the man
who'd just trimmed the wicks of his pards. Before
Avril could get a single shot off, Hawk triggered both
his Russian and his Colt at the same time, carving two
holes, one directly beside the other, in the upper
center of Avril's chest.

He yelped and dropped his pistol, twisting and
raising both forearms to his chest. He threw his head
back as he stumbled around as though drunk, the two
businessmen standing at the bar sidling away from
him. (By now, the other customers were all lying belly
down on the floor, their heads in their arms.) Meanwhile, Johnny awkwardly gained his feet and, crouched

forward, ran in a shambling fashion, dragging his boot toes, out the front batwings, screaming, "Help me— I've been killed!"

He ran off the veranda and into the street, still screaming, "Help me—I've been killed!"

Hawk strode casually across the room in which the gun smoke wafted thickly, and pushed through the batwings. Johnny was out in the middle of the street, staggering and bleeding. Horseback riders and wagon drivers and pedestrians all stopped to stare incredulously at the screaming young man in the gaudy garb of the southwestern border *bandito*.

"Help me!" Johnny screamed again, swinging around to point accusingly toward Hawk. "My name is Johnny Stanley an' that bastard over there done me in! Someone get my father! That bastard killed me!"

"Apparently I haven't yet," Hawk grumbled, stopping on the saloon's front stoop. He raised both pistols, cocked them, aimed, and narrowed his green-eyed gaze down both barrels at once.

The Russian and the Colt bucked and roared simultaneously.

Johnny was punched back off his feet and lay dead, limbs spread out, in the street. The driver of a freight wagon couldn't get his team stopped in time. The heavy rig ran over Johnny and left the young, dead, would-be saloon robber rolling in the dust like an oversized ragdoll.

The freight driver bellowed at his mules, checking them down. Once the wagon had stopped, the driver hitched around in his seat to look at the dead man lying under a cloud of wafting dust behind him.

"I'll be damned," the driver said, running a beefy forearm across his mouth. To no one in particular, he asked, "Ain't that Johnny Stanley?"

The bearded freighter shuttled his shocked gaze from Stanley to Hawk, still standing on the veranda of the Arkansas River Saloon.

"I reckon it *was*," the rogue lawman muttered, holstering both his smoking pistols. "Now at least he's *quiet*." He turned toward the batwings but stopped when he saw a man wearing a five-pointed star walking along the main street, angling toward what remained of Johnny Stanley. The lawman's wary eyes were on Hawk. He had a pistol in his hand, aimed in Hawk's direction.

Hawk winced, then sighed. The lawman was an unwelcome complication. Lifting his hat and running his hand through his hair, Hawk walked back into the saloon while the other customers, looking harried and owly as they collected their valuables, brushed past him on their way out. They sidestepped the rogue lawman as though taking the long way around a stalking panther.

The little barman, Pevney, stood staring wide-eyed toward Hawk. "Is... is he... dead?"

"Unless he can digest lead bettern' most," Hawk said, and returned to his table.

He sat down, finished what whiskey was left in his shot glass, then poured himself another drink. He knew he was due a visit from the local law, so he might

as well wait here and get it out of the way. He didn't
have to wait long. Boots thudded on the veranda. The
lawman looked over the batwings. His eyes found
Hawk, and then he stepped inside, aiming his
Remington out from his right hip, keeping that elbow
close to his belly.

He was an odd-looking gent with an understated,
well-trimmed mustache and a nose that hadn't
received the doctoring it had required.

He stopped inside the batwings and looked at the
two dead men still spilling blood onto the sawdust-
covered puncheons.

Pevney cleared his throat and said haltingly,
"Johnny and his two buddies there, Dave an' Avril
Donnan... they was... tryin' to rob me, Marshal Coates.
Johnny blew out my mirror there. They was..."

He let his voice trail off when Coates stopped and
cast a scowl at him. "Did I ask you a single question,
Joe?"

Pevney just stared at the local lawman, pale-blue
eyes round as saucers.

"Did I?" Coates asked again, louder, tighter.

Joe Pevney shook his head.

"Then kindly shut the fuck up," Coates said.

Pevney swallowed.

Coates walked over to Hawk's table.

"Who're you?"

Hawk lifted his shot glass, sipped his whiskey, and
then set the glass back down on the table. "Hollis.
George Hollis."

"Cold steel artist, eh?"

"Nah. Just a man who don't like to empty his pockets unless it's my own idea."

"Think you're smart, do you?" Coates curled his upper lip. "Well, Hollis, you're in a fine pickle."

Hawk said nothing. He turned to gaze out one of the two windows facing the street on that side of the room. A small crowd had gathered around Johnny Stanley. Several in the crowd were gesticulating wildly.

"Did you hear me, Hollis?"

Hawk turned to Coates. "I heard you. I ain't in no kind of pickle—fine or otherwise. The barman there told you what happened."

Coates glanced over his shoulder at Pevney, who looked sheepish. "I didn't hear a goddamn word that fool said." He turned back to Hawk and gestured with his revolver. "Stand up. Slow."

Hawk sighed. He picked up his shot glass and threw back the rest of his whiskey. Then he slid his chair back too quickly for Coates's taste.

"I said slow, damnit! And get those hands up!"

Slowly, Hawk raised his hands to his shoulders. Slowly, he rose from his chair.

"Now, just as slowly," Coates said, taking a wary step back, "set them pistols on the table."

Hawk set first the Russian, then the Colt on the table.

"Get them hands up!" Coates barked.

Hawk raised his hands to his shoulders.

Coates shoved each of Hawk's pistols down behind his own cartridge belt.

"Now, then," Coates said, waving his cocked

revolver and taking another cautious step backward, "let's go on over to the jail. I'm gonna lock you up and go through my wanted circulars. Just got a fresh batch in off the stage last week."

He gave a shrewd grin. "I got me a suspicion I'll find your half-breed face on one of 'em."

Keeping his hands raised, Hawk walked slowly across the room toward the door, stepping over Dave's bleeding carcass. As he did, Coates bent down behind him, scooped the burlap pouch off the floor, and tossed it over to the wide-eyed Joe Pevney. "Put that away, you damn fool!"

Pevney caught the pouch against his chest, and staggered backward, his eyes on Hawk and Coates.

Hawk pushed through the batwings. He glanced over his shoulder at Coates. The lawman was staying about six feet back behind him, just out of Hawk's reach.

"North," Coates said when Hawk had dropped down the steps and into the street. "Any fast moves, Mister, and I'll drill you right here and leave you to the wild dogs that come into town every night to scavenge."

"All right," Hawk said, heading north along the main street. "Don't be so nervous."

"Nervous, hell!" Coates hurried forward and gave Hawk a hard, angry shove and then stepped back again, out of his prisoner's reach. "You're the one that oughta be nervous. When Mortimer Stanley gets wind of what you done to his boy—his only boy—he's gonna throw a necktie party in your honor!"

Coates chuffed with delight.

As Hawk walked north, he glanced to his left. A box wagon had been drawn up in front of Burt Schweigert's Harness Shop. Several townsmen and even a few women in feathered picture hats stood around, watching as a thin younger man with a limp and a much older, gray-haired gent loaded young Johnny Stanley into the back of the wagon. On a side panel of the wagon had been painted in ornate red lettering CHARLES AND BUSTER McCAULEY UNDERTAKING.

"Well, you made a friend in the McCauleys anyway," Coates said.

When Hawk reached the town marshal's office, he moved up onto the porch. Coates's boots thudded on the steps beside him.

"It's open," Coates said.

Hawk paused in front of the closed door. He turned his head to peer at the crowd still gathered in front of the harness shop. The tall man and the older, gray-haired man were now driving away with Johnny Stanley's body flopping lifelessly in the back, beneath a ratty gray blanket. They were heading for the saloon to pick up the other two cadavers.

"I told you, it's open," Coates said, louder.

"I was just wonderin'," Hawk said.

"Wonderin' what?"

He glanced over his shoulder at Coates, narrowing one eye in speculation. "I never been sure what's appropriate in this situation. Should I send flowers?"

Hawk grinned as he tripped the door's steel latch.

Behind him, Coates's face reddened with anger. He lunged forward, raising his pistol, intending to slam the barrel down against the back of Hawk's head. "You smart-ass son of a—!"

Hawk wheeled quickly right, throwing up his right arm. Coates's gun slammed into it, and fell to the floor of the porch. Coates gave a surprised grunt. Hawk brought up a right haymaker and laid it across the lawman's left cheek with a resounding smack that sent Coates hurtling backward off the porch steps and into the street, where he fell in the dirt on his butt.

Hawk moved down the porch steps as Coates grabbed Hawk's own Colt from behind his cartridge belt and, snarling, raised the revolver and thumbed the hammer back. The gun roared. Hawk kicked it out of the man's hand but not before the bullet had torn into Hawk's upper left arm.

Coates screamed and clutched his injured right wrist in his left hand.

Hawk grabbed the man by his shirt collar, hoisted him up out of the dirt, and pummeled the man's jaws. Coates grunted and dropped to a knee. He fumbled for Hawk's second gun. The rogue lawman pulled his Russian out from behind Coates's cartridge belt, and tossed it away.

He grabbed Coates again by his shirt, lifted him up, and, fury radiating from the raging fire in his wounded left arm, sent four right jabs into Coates's mouth.

The man's lips exploded like ripe tomatoes.

Coates fell in the dirt, spitting blood flecked with

teeth. With the bellowing roar of an incensed grizzly, he hoisted himself up and came at Hawk with both fists flying. Hawk's left arm was useless, but rage was a living thing inside him. Coates managed to land a single right cross on Hawk's left cheek, but Hawk ducked another one and came up slamming his right fist again and again into Coates's ribs.

He could feel bones snap beneath the pummeling.

Hawk kept battering the lawman as Coates stumbled backward, screaming, futilely trying to shield himself from the vicious blows of an enraged, unabashed fighter who outweighed him by twenty pounds. Unlike Coates, who had a doughy midsection, very little of Hawk was anything but taut sinew and bulging muscle.

When Coates crouched to shield his ribs, Hawk hammered the man's ears until they looked like red cauliflowers.

Coates fell on the sun-bleached boardwalk fronting the Wells Fargo office and post office, on the far side of the street from the jail. He lay on the boardwalk, legs curled into the street, breathing hard and wagging his head. He spat more blood. Both eyes were swelling like purple eggs.

"Enough," he said so softly and gratingly that Hawk could barely make it out. "Enough. Fer... chrissakes... *enough*...!"

Hinges squawked.

Hawk looked up. An old man with a long, gray beard and wearing a leather-brimmed cap with the

Wells Fargo insignia sewn into the brim stared warily out through a ten-inch gap in the office door.

The Wells Fargo agent looked from Hawk to the bloodied local lawman writhing like a landed fish on the boardwalk before him. He looked at Hawk again. His gaze slid to Hawk's bloody left arm.

Hawk followed the man's gaze. Blood oozed from a hole about halfway between Hawk's shoulder and elbow. Shit. He'd have to get it sewn up before he left town. There was no telling when he'd find another town... not that he felt inclined to set foot in another one again. Not after his experience in this one, which didn't figure on improving any time soon.

Hawk removed his neckerchief and began wrapping it around his arm. He looked at the old man. "Sawbones hereabouts?"

CHAPTER 6

ARLISS SAT IN ROY'S KITCHEN, SIPPING THE TEA she'd just brewed.

She'd thought that with time she'd come to see the kitchen, the house, as both hers and Roy's. But now, after yesterday's savage attack, she knew she'd never see the house as anyone's but Roy's. Roy's and Charmian's.

Arliss would continue to live here, a stranger, in Roy's and Charmian's house. When she could find somewhere else to go and a way to support herself, she'd pack her bags and leave. Roy and Charmian... the dearly departed Charmian, crawling with worms and maggots in her cold, dark grave... could have the place to themselves.

Until then, Arliss would live here. But she no longer considered herself Roy's wife. If Roy ever considered her his wife again, she'd take the butcher knife down off the wall over the range and geld him with it. That would clarify the situation right well.

She gave a satisfied snort. Then, feeling the burn in her left cheek, which had been scraped raw when he'd taken her atop the table, she brushed her fingers across the scrape, which she'd lightly dabbed with arnica.

"Bastard."

Arliss lifted the tea to her lips once more. She frowned, staring down at the steaming brew. It was missing something...

Arliss got up from the table, walked into the parlor area of the house, and retrieved Roy's bottle of rye from the cabinet by his rocking chair. She returned to the table, sat down, pried the cork out of the bottle with a grunt, and splashed a goodly portion into the tea. She sipped it.

"Mmm," she said, licking her lips. "Better."

She was about to take another sip when she heard a stumbling sound outside. A man was out there, breathing hard, grunting. The stumbling grew louder. She looked at the post where Roy usually kept his spare revolver, the old Remington. It was no longer there, however. He'd probably hid it or taken it with him to the jailhouse after she'd nearly shot him with it yesterday, before he'd raped her.

Arliss froze in her chair, not sure what to do—how to defend herself.

Boots thumped on the stoop and then the knob rattled and the door was shoved open. Roy lurched halfway in; then, one hand remaining on the door-knob, he dropped to his knees. At least, Arliss thought it was Roy. His face looked like a swollen, bloody mask, the lips torn and ragged.

"Arliss!" Roy bellowed throatily, blood dribbling down his chin.

Arliss's heart thudded. She started to rise from her chair, then, feeling a strange, devilish satisfaction, sank back down in the hide seat.

"Arrr-lissss!" Roy bellowed again, louder. He hadn't seen her sitting at the table, only eight feet away from him.

With malevolent casualness, she said, "What happened, Roy? You look like you got run over by an ore wagon." She almost laughed.

Roy jerked his head toward her. His eyes glistened between the swollen lids. He dropped his hand off the doorknob, and said, "Help me upstairs!"

Arliss sipped her whiskey-laced tea and arched a brow at him coolly. "What happened?"

Roy ground his teeth. He spoke as though he had rocks in his mouth. "Will you just get your ass up out of that chair and help me upstairs? Then fetch the doc!"

"Get yourself upstairs."

"Arliss!"

"Get yourself upstairs, Roy."

He looked at her. Then he dropped to all fours with a groan. "Goddamn... goddamn you..."

Arliss slid her chair back and rose. "No. Goddamn you, Roy." She walked around the table and glared down at him. "What happened? The Chain Link boys?" When the boisterous Chain Link hands got drunk on payday, Roy often had trouble controlling them, despite his toughness. He'd had several deputies over the years, but the job didn't pay well enough to compensate for Roy's pugnaciousness, so none had lasted long and Roy had given up on trying to fill the position.

He shook his weary head. He was looking at the floor. "You help me upstairs, I'll tell you." He glanced up at her through his swollen eyelids. "I'll tell you about your brother."

Arliss frowned. So her brother had something to do with this. Somehow, she wasn't surprised. When there was trouble in town or in the county, Johnny usually had some part in it. He'd been running off his leash for the past several years.

Arliss no longer had any sisterly feelings for Johnny, but out of mild curiosity, and because she wanted to get Roy out of her hair, she grabbed his arm and helped him to his feet. She struggled to get him upstairs and into the room she now considered to be his alone. His and Charmian's.

After yesterday, Arliss had moved into the spare bedroom—the room originally intended for Roy and Charmian's child, which, because Charmian had been barren, had never materialized.

Arliss got Roy on the bed. He lay huffing and puffing and grunting in agony.

"Whiskey," Roy groaned, glancing at the whiskey bottle on the small, round table near the upholstered armchair in the corner.

The table sat beneath the bright, oval-shaped spot

in the otherwise sun-faded wallpaper that marked where the tintype wedding photograph of Roy and Charmian had been hanging until Arliss had moved in and taken it down.

Arliss poured whiskey into the glass. She held the glass out to Roy. When he reached for it, she jerked it back.

"Johnny," she said.

Roy scowled up at her, shifting his smoldering gaze between her and the whiskey that shone a pretty amber in a ray of sunlight angling through a near window.

"Dead," he said, snidely. He almost smiled.

She felt her lower jaw loosen. She didn't know why she was surprised. She'd always figured her brother would end up killed in one of the dustups he was always getting involved in. Still, the information took her off-guard. Johnny gone. She didn't feel any emotion about the loss, for she and Johnny had been alienated for years. Still, the world suddenly seemed a little stranger than it had a moment ago.

Roy reached for the glass. Again, Arliss pulled it away.

"Did you kill him?" she asked.

"Hell, no." Roy chuckled without mirth. "He was tryin' to rob the Arkansas. Some stranger shot him and those two worthless trail pards of his."

"What happened to you?"

"The stranger resisted arrest." Roy stretched his lips back with a grimace, then grabbed the glass out of Arliss's hand before she could pull it away again. He scowled down into the glass and said through a snarl, "He got his, though. I put a bullet in him."

Roy tossed back half the whiskey in the glass. Pulling the glass down, he smacked his lips and gave a phlegmy sigh. "Just wait till your pa hears about this." He shook his head fatefully. "Hell's gonna pop. That firebrand could do no wrong in old Mort Stanley's eyes. The more shit he pulled... the more men he killed... your pa just puffed his chest out a little bigger."

Arliss was deep in thought, staring down at the bed. She jerked when Roy barked, *"Fetch the doc, goddamnit. My ribs need settin'!"*

Arliss shot him a withering glare. "You go to hell!"

She swung around, stomped out of the room, and drew the door closed behind her.

"Arliss, you fetch the doc!" Roy yelled on the other side of the door. His tone grew desperate, wheedling. "I told you I was sorry about what happened yesterday. I was in a real bad mood. I won't ever do it again. You fetch the doc, now—all right, honey?"

She strode into the smaller room at the end of the hall and sat on the edge of her bed. She folded her hands in her lap and stared out the curtained window at a cottonwood branch. She could hear Roy's labored breathing edged with frequent groans on the other side of the wall.

She sat there for maybe a minute, pondering. Coming to a decision about what she would do, she got up, grabbed her felt riding hat and her gloves and light wool jacket, and left the room. As she dropped down the stairs, her heels clicking on the uncarpeted steps, Roy yelled from behind his closed door, "God-damnit, Arliss, you fetch the doc for me, you contrary bitch!"

Arliss went out and drew the front door closed behind her.

She strode out of the yard and traced the shortest route to the heart of town, where Doctor Donleavy housed his practice. She hadn't intended to fetch a doctor for Roy. He deserved to suffer. But then she realized that his suffering would only make her suffer more. Best get him patched up and out of the house as soon as possible.

"You lookin' fer the doc, Miss Arliss?" asked George Howe, who was arranging hoes and other hand implements in a barrel outside Howe's Mercantile. Arliss had started up the outside stairs that gave access to the doctor's office in the mercantile's second story.

Howe gave a weak, knowing smile. He knew she was fetching the doctor for Roy.

Arliss stopped three steps up from the bottom of the stairs. "Is he in?"

Howe shook his head and shuttled his somewhat sheepish gaze kitty-corner across the street. "He's over at the hotel. Whitehall fetched him a half hour ago."

"Oh," Arliss said, puzzled. "All right."

She glanced at Howe once more, then headed across the street to the Colorado Hotel.

"Sorry about Johnny, Miss Arliss," Howe called behind her, smiling weakly.

"No, you're not, Mister Howe," Arliss said over her

shoulder. She doubted that anyone in the county would miss Johnny Stanley. She doubted she'd miss him. At least, she wouldn't miss the firebrand he'd been for the past five years. The only one who'd miss him was their father.

She went into the hotel and learned from Chester Whitehall, the hotelier, that the doctor was tending a patient on the second floor, in room nine. Arliss climbed the stairs to the second floor, and knocked on the door of room nine. She hadn't realized the door wasn't latched. Her first knock nudged it open far enough that she could see a gun being jerked in a blur of fast motion from a holster. The gun was cocked and aimed at her.

Arliss gasped, then froze.

She looked up from the gun to the face of the man wielding it. Her heart fluttered, and her mouth went dry. The doctor, who stood beside the man sitting on the bed aiming the pistol at her, turned toward her, wide-eyed. He'd been wrapping the knuckles of the sitting man's right hand with a white flannel bandage. The sitting man's upper left arm was also wrapped. A spot of red shone on it.

The sitting man's torso was bare.

Arliss remembered looking up at that same bare chest as it hovered over her. She remembered the masculine smell of it, the sensation of the man's slab-like muscles against her kneading hands as he'd toiled between her legs.

"Arliss...?" the doctor said.

The sitting man depressed his revolver's hammer.

He lowered the gun to the bed and stared at her, expressionless. His green eyes burned in deep sockets. They threatened to mesmerize her.

Arliss tore her gaze away from his. She cleared her throat, swallowed, and looked at the doctor. "I just wanted to let you know that Roy could use some tending, too, Doc."

Doctor Donleavy was tall and gaunt with a beak-like nose and pewter-gray hair combed to one side, a rooster tail licking up at the top of his head. He blinked his somber eyes, and said, "I don't doubt that he does. Is he home?"

Arliss nodded.

The doctor said, "I'll head over to your place just as soon as I'm done here. Only be another minute or two."

Arliss nodded. She glanced once more at the man on the bed. He stared at her with the same blank expression as before. Again, her heart fluttered. She looked at the bandage on his arm, then at the hand the doctor was wrapping. She could see that the knuckles were scraped and bloody.

As he continued to wrap the sitting man's hand, Donleavy looked at her again. "Was there something else, Arliss?"

Arliss shook her head and turned away.

She walked down the hotel stairs and stepped out onto the front veranda. She pressed her hands to the rail and leaned forward, breathless. Of course, she hadn't forgotten about the stranger, but she hadn't expected to see him here in town. She certainly hadn't expected their paths to cross in this way.

No, nothing like this.

Johnny was dead and Roy was home in bed, badly beaten by the man she'd...

Arliss turned to look up at the hotel's second story. She gazed at the window of what she thought was room nine. She found herself strangely drawn to it. To *him*—to the man who'd killed her brother and beat her husband half to death.

Who was he? What was he doing here? How was it that he had come out of nowhere to so quickly and improbably affect her life in such a large way?

Arliss turned to stare out into the street. Several townsmen and townswomen were walking past the hotel. They saw her standing on the hotel veranda, and they stared, obviously having heard that her notorious brother had been killed. They were wondering how she was taking the news. Most importantly, however, they were likely wondering how her father would take the news.

Johnny dead.

Arliss still couldn't quite wrap her mind around that fact herself. But a fact it was. She wasn't sure why, but she felt the need to be the one to tell her father. She certainly didn't owe it to him to be the one. He deserved to be told by someone outside the family. By one of his several agents in town. Maybe that's what he'd prefer, in fact. Maybe, if she told him, he'd realize that a large part of her motivation was to rub his nose in it.

So what if he did?

Arliss dropped down the veranda steps and headed over to the furniture store that doubled as Charles and Buster McCauleys' undertaking business. The shed in which the undertaking took place was behind the main store. Arliss walked through the store cluttered with mostly rough-hewn, handmade furniture toward the shed in the back. Mrs. McCauley was sitting in a chair behind the cluttered rear counter—a strangely masculine-looking woman wearing a green visor as she flipped through a ledger book, a pen in her ink-stained fingers.

She looked at Arliss but said nothing, her eyes grim, her thin mouth turned down at the corners.

Arliss walked out the main store's back door and found Charles and Buster in the undertaking shed. The elder McCauley was rolling a cigarette as Buster, taller and leaner than his father, and walking with a limp he'd been born with, fitted a lid onto one of the two caskets that were propped on sawhorses. Both men jerked with starts as Arliss walked into the shed and stopped between the open double doors. Charles jerked with a more violent start than Buster, dropping his cigarette and makings sack on the shed's earthen floor.

"Lordy, you gave us a fright, Miss Stan... I mean, Mrs. Coates!"

"I came to see my brother." Arliss nodded at the casket that Buster was standing next to. He'd taken a stumbling step back when Arliss had appeared so unexpectedly. "Is that him there?"

CHAPTER 7

REMEMBERING HIS MANNERS, CHARLES MCCAULEY doffed his hat and held it over his heart. "We're so sorry for your loss, Miss Arliss—Buster an' me is, an' the missus, too of course."

"Is that him there?" Arliss asked again, staring at the coffin.

Buster looked at his father.

Charles said, "Yes, it is. We just got him laid out and ready to be planted. Where would you...?"

"I want to see him." Arliss walked toward the diamond-shaped coffin.

Charles stepped forward, as well. "Oh, you wouldn't want to see him, Miss Arliss," the elder McCauley said tenderly. "He's shot up awful bad, and a freight... well, a freight wagon rolled over him."

Arliss looked at Buster. "Open it."

Buster looked from Arliss to his father. Arliss kept her commanding gaze on him.

Charles sighed. "Well, all right, then." He and

Buster pried up the coffin lid, and removed it. They held it between them, stepping back as though to give Arliss some room with her brother.

Arliss stepped up beside the coffin and closed her hands over the edge. She looked down at her brother glaring up at her. Arliss heard herself give an involuntarily groan of revulsion at the hideous sight.

"See, now," Charles said, stepping forward again with the coffin lid. "I told you that ain't somethin' you need to—"

Arliss held up her hand. "Give me a minute!"

Charles stopped. He and Buster shared a look.

Arliss drew a deep breath and looked down once more at her brother. Johnny lay with his hands crossed on his belly. He was a bloody mess. His face was relaxed but his eyes were open as though maintaining the same expression as when Johnny had realized he'd been killed. It was as though he were still staring at the man who'd killed him.

The man in room nine of the Colorado Hotel.

Arliss was a little surprised to feel no sadness about her brother's demise. She was shocked to see him lying here, but only because he'd cut such a broad swath for such a long time, been such a big story around here for so many years, that he'd grown to myth-like proportions.

She also felt a little sheepish and it took her a minute, searching her feelings, to realize that her guilt stemmed from the fact that she'd lain with the man who'd killed him, and enjoyed it. As if that somehow made her complicit in Johnny's death.

Which, of course, it did not.

No, there was no reason for her to feel guilty. She did, however, feel repelled now by the man she'd lain with. By the man in room nine. He'd caused the crumpled, bloody, glaring mess before her... the mess that had once been a living, breathing man.

True, that man had turned sour years ago and become a blight on the county. Still, he'd been alive. And the man in room nine had killed him.

Obviously, what Arliss had suspected about that man was true.

He was a killer. Likely, a hired killer. A shootist. One who'd been holing up in the mountains, likely trying to stave off the punishment due from recent transgressions not unlike the one glaring up at Arliss now.

A killer. She'd lain with a killer. The killer of her brother.

And she'd enjoyed it.

In fact, she hadn't been able to get that night out of her mind. She'd found herself thinking about it even more intensely after Roy had raped her. Odd, how two such similar acts could have such dissimilar effects.

One had caused her to feel in a way she hadn't known was possible.

The other had been torture. Because of it, she'd vowed she'd never let Roy touch her again. She'd kill herself first.

Arliss stared down at her dead brother.

No, she didn't feel any sadness. Even her guilt was quickly diminishing, now that she knew there was no cause for it. The feeling moving in to replace it was one of... what?

Satisfaction.

Johnny's death was proof—as though any was needed—that their father was a monster. And Arliss couldn't wait to show the man the irrefutable evidence.

Mortimer Stanley had turned Johnny into what he'd become, and he'd turned his only daughter over to the town marshal of Cedar Bend as a bribe, keeping the lawman in his pocket. Another reason he'd forced her into marriage with a man she hadn't loved was to simply be rid of her. He hadn't wanted her on the ranch anymore, reminding him how her brother had turned out. He especially hadn't wanted her around after Arliss had seen what she'd seen, what she knew about the death of her mother.

Arliss looked at Charles and Buster McCauley staring at her curiously, holding the coffin lid vertically between them.

"I'm going to need your wagon," she said. "I'm going to take my brother home to our father."

The McCauleys shared another dubious look.

———

AN HOUR LATER, ARLISS SAT IN THE DRIVER'S SEAT OF the undertakers' wagon, staring up at two dead men hanging over the trail. Each man wore a noose around his neck. Both ropes had been tied off near the bottom of the pine tree from which the two men hung, twisting slowly in opposite directions in the mountain breeze.

Each was dressed in drover's attire typical of the area—wool shirts, neckerchief, vests, and brush-scarred chaps over faded denims, the denim nearly worn through on the insides of the thighs. The marks of men who spent most of their days in the saddle, riding for the brand.

One man wore a beard. His hair was long, thick, and tangled.

The other wore a two- or three-day growth of beard stubble. He was blond, with a broad face and misshapen nose. The death grimace twisting his lips showed several missing teeth. His name was Early. He'd grown up in these mountains. Arliss had seen him out on the range when she was still living at home, and, more recently, she'd seen him in town. Last time she'd seen him, he'd been driving her father's supply wagon. He'd worked for her father as a ranch hand.

She didn't recognize the bushy-headed drover, but he'd likely worked for Mortimer Stanley, as well. They'd been hanged here together, on the Circle S range. Their faces were badly cut and swollen. They'd each been given a savage beating not unlike the one Roy had taken. Their shirts were torn and soiled.

Arliss grimaced, then shook the reins over the back of the gelding in the traces. She continued on up the trail that would take her to her father's ranch headquarters. Pines stood tall on both sides of the trail, at times nearly blocking out the sky. The trail followed the course of an old ravine. The route became impassable during the rainy season and during the spring snowmelt, making travel to town impossible for at least two months out of every year.

Arliss knew that fact very well—and the closed-in feeling it had given her every year she'd lived out here, having been born on the ranch. The closed-in feeling hadn't been such a bad thing, however. It had been a fact of life, and she'd come to even enjoy the feeling of living on an island of sorts.

Besides, she'd been happy most of those years. This was back before four years ago, before her mother had died and everything had gone to hell, including her father and her brother.

And herself, as well.

Now everything was changed. The ravine trail looked dark and menacing to her today, as it curved slowly up the mountain to the pass on the other side of which lay the ranch in a broad, grassy bowl along the North Fork of Diamond Creek. Home to her once. Now she felt as though she were on the trail to hell.

She was maybe two hundred yards from the top of the pass when a pistol cracked in the forest somewhere around her. The report echoed hollowly. It was followed by one more blast and the ensuing echoes.

Arliss's heart lurched. The gelding whickered testily.

"Hold up!" a man shouted. Because of the echoes, it was hard to tell, but Arliss thought the voice had come from her right.

She stared up the slope on that side of the trail.

Her eyes picked out movement in the forms of two horseback riders coming down the slope, their horses picking their way, tails arched. The men rode out onto the trail ahead of Arliss, turned toward her, and reined up.

One of the horses whinnied and shook its head.

The gelding pulling the undertakers' wagon whinnied in kind.

The men stared grimly out from beneath the brims of their weather-stained Stetsons. It didn't take long, however, before both sets of eyes acquired the glassy cast of male lust. They looked at each other, smirking, and rode forward.

"Well, now," one of them said, approaching the wagon.

He opened his mouth to continue, but Arliss cut him off with, "I'm Arliss Coates. Your employer's daughter, if you ride for Stanley. And since that's the Stanley Circle S brand on both your horses, you do. Unless you're horse thieves, that is." She didn't recognize either man. That wasn't unusual. She hadn't been out here since she'd been married off to Roy, and her father's payroll was forever changing.

Both men sobered up quickly. They gave each other a quick conferring glance, and the first one said, "Oh, well, we're sorry if we spooked you, Miss Arliss. Mister Stanley's given the order we should check everyone we see out here. Rustlin' has been a problem of late."

"Oh?" Arliss said. "Who'd be foolish enough to rustle Stanley beef? Doesn't everyone know my father's reputation for not tolerating long-looping by now?"

"You'd think so," said the second rider, hiking a shoulder. "But..."

Arliss hooked a thumb over her shoulder. "What about those two decorating that pine tree back there? I recognized one as Lyle Early."

"That's Early, all right," said the first rider. He was a small, lean rider in a pinto vest and funnel-brimmed hat. He also had two smart-looking pistols on his hips. "Your pa thinks him and Newton was stealin' beef right out from under his nose."

"What do you think?" Arliss asked him, blocking the sun from her eyes with her gloved right hand.

The small, lean rider glanced at the other man—a tall man with a long, angular face covered with a cinnamon beard streaked with gray. He wore two pistols in shoulder rigs. He shrugged and grinned without humor at Arliss. "Like your pa tells us every morning before he sends us out on the range, we ain't paid to think, Miss Arliss. We're paid to work."

He grinned again. Then he glanced into the wagon box. "Who's that?"

"My brother."

Both men stared at her, their eyes widening, pupils expanding. They didn't seem to know how to respond to the information. They'd obviously known Johnny. They probably knew what a close relationship Johnny had had with their father.

They probably knew how the old man would take the news of Johnny's demise, as well.

The infamous Johnny Stanley...

"Well, if you two will excuse me," Arliss said, lifting her reins in her hand.

"We'll ride point for you, Miss Arliss," said the smaller man, turning his horse around and starting up the trail. "A purty girl shouldn't be travelin' alone out here!" He threw up an arm, beckoning.

The news had energized both men. Arliss knew from her own experience how any news, even bad news, could excite those who dwelled this far off the beaten path. The news of the demise of Johnny Stanley, welcome news to some, unwelcome news to others —namely, Mortimer Stanley—was nevertheless big news indeed.

They both galloped on up toward the pass, their yells echoing off the surrounding slopes.

Arliss shook the reins over the gelding's back. The wagon lurched up the trail, over the pass, down the other side, and into the yard of the Stanley Circle S.

CHAPTER 8

ARLISS WATCHED THE DROVERS ANGLE THEIR HORSES over to the bunkhouse, which sat next to the breaking corral and one of the headquarters' two barns. As the riders pulled their horses up in front of the bunkhouse, the door opened and several men ducked out onto the stoop to join the three men who were already sitting there, smoking.

They were a ragged-looking lot. Long-haired, scraggly-bearded, mean-eyed, and dirty. They also wore guns—even the one who sat on the stoop, kicked back in his hide-bottom chair wearing only his balbriggans, hat. and boots.

No one seemed to be working. It was the middle of the week, but all of the hands appeared to be sticking close to the bunkhouse. The bleary cast to their gazes told Arliss they'd been drinking. Not working. Drinking.

Was it a holiday?

Puzzled, she looked around the ranch yard—at the

tack shed, at the blacksmith shack, whose doors were closed, as if no one had been working there so far today; at the two corrals in addition to the breaking corral, and at the springhouse and the windmill and the stock tank ringing the base of it.

Aside from the men now standing or lounging around outside the bunkhouse, staring at Arliss dubiously, the place could have been deserted. The buildings looked rundown and unoccupied. Weeds had grown up around all three corrals. A corral gate hung askew. Several shake shingles were missing from the roof of the blacksmith shack. Both barns needed the chinking replaced between their stout logs, and they needed the weeds cut down along their stone foundations.

The dozen or so horses milling in the corrals needed currying.

Arliss cast her gaze up the rise to the south. Her heart fell at the shape the main house was in. Her father had built the place soon after he'd established the ranch, after he'd spent his first two years out here alone in a small, one-room log shanty he'd built himself.

Mortimer Stanley had taken pride in the building of the house, which resembled a manor house from the Antebellum South he'd taken his leave of several years before the war had broken out. Not long after he'd moved their mother out here, they'd welcome their first baby—their one and only boy, Johnny. Three years later, Arliss had come along.

They were a small family for such a large house,

but Arliss had enjoyed the vast, airy rooms with their rich furnishings shipped to these mountains from places like Kansas City and New Orleans. Her father's initial investment in a Texas herd had paid off richly nearly right away, for he'd found a lucrative market for his beef in nearby mining camps and boomtowns.

Arliss had been happy here. For her first fifteen years, anyway...

The house now stood atop the southern rise, a steep, forested ridge looming behind it—an affront to her fond memory of the place. The house's clapboards and colonnade fronting the veranda badly needed paint. Shutters hung askew. Some were missing altogether. Weeds and brush grew thick inside the picket fence that also needed paint or replacing altogether. Some of the boards, including the entire front gate, looked entirely rotten. They were the color of soiled rags.

Arliss glanced toward the men on the bunkhouse porch. She didn't recognize any of them. They must have all been hired since she'd left here two years ago, married off to the town marshal of Cedar Bend. She wanted to find a familiar face, and ask him what had happened. Was her father dead? But she saw no one she felt inclined to speak with. They all eyed her curiously but also vaguely menacingly. Some had outright lust in their drink-rheumy eyes.

Arliss shook the reins over the gelding's back. The horse pulled the wagon up the rise and onto the cinder-paved drive forming a turnaround before the rotting trellis fronting the picket fence. The trellis was covered with dead vines tufted with dead, dried-up leaves that made dry rasping sounds in the breeze that kicked up dust around the hill.

Arliss set the brake and wrapped the reins around it.

She glanced at the house once more. Apprehension plucked at her. The house not only looked deserted, but haunted. She was half afraid she'd find her father dead inside, moldering, while his hands had been scavenging the place, drinking in the bunkhouse.

She climbed off the wagon and patted the gelding's neck. She looked down the rise toward the bunkhouse. The men were still standing out there, gazing at her. She turned away and pushed her way through the vines choking the trellis, through the front gate, and into the yard. She stopped when she saw a figure move out of the square shadow of the front door, and step out onto the broad veranda.

Arliss stopped with a start, slapping her hand to her chest.

She studied the tall, stoop-shouldered man with wild, thin, curly gray hair growing like a tumbleweed around his long, caved-in face. Mortimer Stanley leaned against one of the veranda's rotting wooden columns as though he needed propping up. He wore a ratty robe over balbriggans. He wore stovepipe, mule-eared boots, and a gun holstered on his left thigh.

In his right hand, hanging down low by his side, was a bottle.

"Father..." Arliss said, a little breathless. He looked

as though he'd been ill. He hadn't shaved in days. His skin looked pasty and oily.

"Damn." Stanley lifted the bottle to his lips, taking a drink. Swallowing, he said, "You're purtier'n a speckled pup. I always did say that."

Arliss couldn't bring herself to say anything. She was in shock at the state of the place. At the state of her father. Suddenly, she wished she hadn't come. She felt as though she were living one of those nightmares that occur just before waking, in which you find all the landmarks of your life in ruins, and all is lost. You awaken from such dreams, reeling a bit, but relieved that you'd only been dreaming.

Only now she wasn't dreaming.

Mort Stanley studied her through only vaguely familiar eyes, and when she didn't say something, he glanced at the wagon and said, "Who you got there?"

Arliss cleared her throat. Her tongue felt thick. She suddenly didn't feel the gloating satisfaction she'd felt on her way up here with the body of the brother whose life her father had ruined.

"Your son."

"What?"

Arliss glanced slowly back at the wagon, then turned to her father once more. His eyes came alive with concern as he pushed away from the column. He set the bottle down on the veranda floor, got his boots set beneath him, and, looking at Arliss with a suspicious, troubled expression, came down the steps heavily, shamble-footed, and strode uncertainly down the stone walk.

He brushed past Arliss, pushed through the vines threatening to seal up the trellis, and walked over to the wagon. He looked down at the coffin for a time, his hands on the wagon's side panels.

Arliss watched his shoulders rise and fall as he breathed, staring down in dread at the sanded pine box.

Finally, he glanced over his shoulder at Arliss once more, then walked around to the end of the wagon. He climbed inside, grunting and sighing, his face flushing with the effort. He stood over the casket, facing Arliss, his back to the ranch yard and the men watching from the bunkhouse.

He dropped to his knees. He was breathing even harder than before. His face was red-splotched and swollen, and his lips were parted. He dug his fingers under the edge of the lid, pried up the cover, and tossed it aside. It thudded loudly to the floor of the wagon.

Mortimer Stanley stared down at the body of his son glaring up at him.

"Oh," Stanley said, throwing his arms up and out from his sides in a weird pantomime of a slow hug. "Oh," he said again, his voice pinching and his lips pooching out as sobs overcame him. "Oh... oh, god!"

Mortimer Stanley lowered his arms and lifted Johnny's torso out of the coffin. He hugged his son tight to his chest, pressing his left cheek against the side of Johnny's head, and bawled. His dead son hung slack in his arms, Johnny's open eyes glaring into space over his father's left shoulder.

From where Arliss stood in the yard, she could look out over the ranch yard below. Her father's men were all standing in front of the bunkhouse now, staring this way.

Stanley sobbed and howled over his dead boy's slack body.

Finally, he dropped the body back into the coffin. He drew a deep breath, snot and saliva dribbling off his nose and lips. He squeezed his eyes closed, shook his head, said, "Oh, god!" and then crouched over the coffin once more.

He drew Johnny out of the pine box and, crouching uncertainly, pulled the body up over his right shoulder. Arliss wasn't sure how he managed it—she felt certain he'd topple over the side of the wagon and break his neck—but he climbed out of the back of the wagon with Johnny hanging slack over his right shoulder.

Stanley must have been stronger than he looked, though as he passed Arliss on the cracked stone walk, he staggered badly, sobbing, his breath rasping in and out of his tired, old lungs. Arliss watched him negotiate the broad veranda steps and then disappear into the dark house that stood like a specter of its former self.

Arliss stood there on the walk, wanting to give her father some time alone with Johnny. She felt hollowed out and dull and very, very alone. This day had been a shock to her mind, though of course it had really started yesterday when Roy had raped her on their kitchen table. What was happening now seemed like the natural, dark progression of the bad time that had started twenty-four hours ago. Or maybe it had started even earlier.

Maybe it had really started two nights ago, when the stranger had rescued her from the lake and they'd coupled like wild wolves on that stony ledge above the dark water...

The raucous patter of off-key piano chords jerked Arliss out of her reverie. They caromed out the front door like the volleys of some strange-sounding pistol, reverberating gratingly. The notes softened slightly, and her father's voice sang:

> *"Sowing in the morning,*
> *Sowing seeds of kindness,*
> *Waiting for the harvest and the time of*
>   *reaping,*
> *We shall come rejoicing, bringing in the*
>   *sheaves."*

Arliss glowered through the half-open front door. As her father continued singing the old song, starting the refrain, she walked up the veranda's moldering steps and continued through the front door.

> *"Bringing in the sheaves, bringing in the*
>   *sheaves,*
> *We shall come rejoicing, bringing in the*
>   *sheaves..."*

Arliss followed the unruly piano hammering and

the loud, flat, drunken singing through the broad foyer. The parlor opened to the right, through a set of open French doors. She noted that two of the panes in one of the doors had been broken out, and the glass was still on the floor. Another pane was cracked diagonally. She moved slowly, tentatively, through the opening and into the carpeted foyer with its heavy leather furniture and bookshelves.

The grand piano sat in the room's far corner, just beyond the cold stone hearth of the large fireplace. The Confederate flag was still draped over the top of the piano, as it had been all the years Arliss had grown up here in this too-grand house.

Now her brother's body lay atop the flag, atop the piano, glaring up at the ceiling.

Johnny's arms were flung out to each side. His boots hung down over the piano's near edge. His legs bobbed a little as Mortimer Stanley continued to whack violently at the piano keys, leaning forward and singing loudly, crazily, and with obvious emotion, tears rolling down his sallow cheeks.

> *"Sowing in the sunshine, sowing in the*
> *shadows,*
> *Fearing neither clouds nor winter's chilling*
> *breeze,*
> *By and by the harvest, and the labor ended,*
> *We shall come rejoicing, bringing in the*
> *sheaves."*

Arliss moved slowly into the room and sat on the

edge of the overstuffed leather couch angled before the cold, stone fireplace. She placed her hands in her lap and tucked her feet close together beneath her. She stared with solemn incredulity at the drunken ghost of a man her father had become, wishing she could feel more satisfaction at the wicked turn his life had taken.

Stanley had just started the refrain again when he stopped, then hammered the keys violently, the notes thundering out of the piano and making Johnny's lifeless head wag from side to side. Stanley dropped his head and sobbed for a long time. Finally, he lifted his head, ran his hands through his hair, and then turned his wet gaze to his daughter.

He didn't say anything. He just stared through those tear-flooded eyes, his face a mask of terrible agony. It was as though he were silently imploring her for an antidote to his malaise. Again, Arliss wished she could take some satisfaction in his pain, after all the pain that he had caused his family. But she could not. All she could feel now for the man she hated even more than Roy Coates was befuddlement at his unexpected turn, and pity.

She looked around the dusty, cluttered room, then shuttled her gaze back to her father and shook her head slowly, uncomprehendingly. "What the hell has happened here, Father? What have you become?" She lifted her chin toward a front window. "Who are those men out there, and why aren't they out on the range, working your cattle?"

Stanley drew a long breath, swept first the back of

one hand across his face, wiping away tears, then the other one. "I need 'em here. The range is infested with rustlers. Mostly from other ranchers pushin' their way in. These mountains are crawlin' with men wantin' to take me down."

"Really?" Arliss found that hard to believe. She knew her father had once had some trouble with rustlers, but most ranchers in these mountains had respected her father's prominence as the first stockman here, and steered clear of the Circle S. "What about Early and the other man—your men—I saw hanging from a tree down on the main trail?"

Stanley shrugged. "Rustlers, both. Stealin' my cows. A few at a time. Harder to miss 'em that way, the beef." He gave a shrewd wink. "They were buildin' their own herd—their own *stolen* herd, *my* herd—to start their own spread or to sell to the railroad, or maybe the Ute reserve."

"Lyle Early?" Arliss found that even harder to believe than the notion that other men were crowding her father. "He was on your role a long time. Why would he suddenly—?"

"That's just it." Stanley rose, glanced down at his dead son adorning the piano, then walked over to a liquor cabinet resting beneath a trophy elk head that had turned gray with dust. Cobwebs clung to its horns. "He figured I trusted him. That's how it always works. The ones you trust most"—facing the wall, he threw back a shot of brandy, then turned slowly to face his daughter—"are the ones you gotta watch."

"Like Mother."

Stanley narrowed his eyes at his daughter, then lifted his mouth corners a little.

"A shrewd, cunning wench—eh, Father?" Arliss curled her upper lip. Her eyes blazed. "Looking for any advantage over you. Took the first opportunity that presented itself to step out on you."

Still, Stanley said nothing. He stood there staring at her with that bizarre half-grin on his wasted face.

Arliss shook her head. "She had no intention of doing what she did. I know she didn't. She couldn't help herself. You were... are... a cold, cold man. Your ranch always came first. And you were rough on her. Too rough. She wasn't like you. She was a sweet Southern belle. I'm more like you. I can take life a little rougher. But Mother was a romantic. She needed love. Tender love from a man who genuinely loved her."

"I loved her," Stanley said stubbornly.

"You don't know the meaning of the word."

Crimson smudged Stanley's cheeks. "Don't you talk to me that way!" He canted his head toward the piano. "Who killed your brother? That's all I want to hear out of your mouth. Then you can ride on back to town."

"No." Arliss shook her head with her father's own kind of stubborn. "I want you to hear this, because I've been wanting to get it off of my chest for a long time."

CHAPTER 9

"Say it, then," Stanley barked at his daughter. "Say it, if it means so goddamn much to you to beat a man when he's down! Your own father! Go ahead!"

His angry, bellowing voice echoed throughout the house.

Arliss's heart had quickened against the familiar attack—the burning eyes and thundering voice. She swallowed, welcomed the burn of anger once more radiating out from the base of her spine, but kept the wave of emotion under control.

She said, "He was a man to her—Richard Neeley. He was a good, kind man to her. I saw the moment they fell in love. It was just after Neeley had moved to the mountains and established his own ranch—in partnership with you, of course—at the base of Dead Man's Forge. He and his foreman had come for Christmas dinner. It was Neeley's sixth or seventh visit. It was that night—the one I'm talking about—when I suddenly realized he hadn't come to talk business with *you*. It was to see *her*. I saw the way they looked at one another. They'd fallen in love!"

Stanley stood glaring at his daughter, lips bunched, a vein bulging in his left temple. He was squeezing his empty goblet in his right hand, down low by his right thigh.

Arliss continued: "I came upon them that spring. They'd met in a glade by Roberts Creek. I was horrified, of course. I'd never seen such a thing—let alone my own mother with another man. In that way."

Stanley's eyes widened. "You saw them?"

Arliss smiled, nodding. "I was horrified at first." Her smile broadened. "And then I was happy for her. Finally, she had found love."

"You bitch! You knew and you didn't tell me! You *bitch*!"

Arliss clenched her hands into fists beside her on the couch, steeling herself against his wrath, and said, "I was terrified when I realized you suspected something about Mother's frequent rides into the countryside, not returning for several hours. I prayed god would not let you follow her, but that day that you did... I followed *you* as you followed *them*."

Arliss felt her lips quiver as the dam of her emotions began to rupture.

"I wanted so badly to get around you and to find her... *them*... before you did... but you were too far ahead... and you were riding too fast. You rode right up to that little woodcutter's shack they'd been meeting in."

Arliss closed her eyes as tears oozed from them. She

didn't want to remember any more about that day, but the images flowed across her mind until she was there, in the woods by the little stream that muttered around the south side of the ancient woodcutter's cabin, long abandoned, that had become her mother's and Richard Neeley's meeting place.

She crossed the stream and stopped her horse. She stared in shock as her father dismounted his cream stallion about thirty yards from the cabin's front door, and dropped the reins.

Stanley jerked up the flap of his coat, unsheathed his revolver, and strode toward the shack. His shoulders were tight, his stride resolute, angry.

"No!" Arliss wanted to scream. "No, Father. No!"

But it seemed as though her vocal chords had dissolved in her throat.

Just then she heard a woman's loud groaning laugh seep out between the unchinked logs of the shack. Arliss hadn't yet made love at that point in her life, but she knew instinctively what that sound had been—her mother's love cry.

Her father stopped abruptly. Her stared as though stricken at the shack.

"No, Father!" Arliss had tried to scream, sitting frozen to her saddle. "No, Father. No, no, no, no!"

Stanley continued forward. He kicked in the dilapidated door, ducked through the low opening, and disappeared into the shack's deep shadows.

A woman screamed.

Neeley shouted, "My god—nooo!"

A gun popped twice. Then a third time. A fourth, a fifth... a sixth.

Arliss had sat her horse so tensely, her bones ached. Her

eyes were squeezed shut. She jerked with each hollow-sounding blast erupting inside the shack.

There were garbled choking sounds.

Arliss opened her eyes just as her father ducked his head to walk out of the shack. He strode over to where his cream stallion stood, whickering nervously. Mort Stanley did not look toward Arliss, who sat her horse about forty yards from him, her figure no doubt obscured by trees and branches. He seemed in a trance as he grabbed his reins and swung into the leather.

He guided his horse around to ride back the way he'd come. Only then did he see his daughter staring in wide-eyed terror at the cabin. He stopped the stallion, jerking back on the reins and regarding Arliss in shock, his face flushed crimson. He sat his prancing stallion for nearly a full minute before, apparently finding no words, he kicked the cream into a gallop.

Horse and rider dashed past Arliss, crossed the stream, and hammered back in the direction of the Circle S.

Moans and sobs rose from inside the shack. There were scuffing sounds, as well. Arliss's mother appeared in the doorway. Naked and bloody, she crouched under the weight of Richard Neeley, whom she seemed to be trying to help exit the shack. She was holding Neeley's right arm around her neck. Her own left arm was around the bloody man's waist. Neeley's head was down. Blood dribbled from his mouth and onto the shack's earthen floor.

The skin of both appeared parchment white behind the blood that seemed to cover them nearly entirely.

"Help!" Arliss's mother cried, sobbing. "Someone... please, help us!"

She managed to make it outside with Richard Neeley, but

then Neeley collapsed and Arliss's mother collapsed on top of him. They lay groaning and sobbing together for what seemed a long time, but must have been only a minute or two.

Neeley fell still. A few seconds later, Arliss's mother fell still, as well.

They lay entangled in each other's arms—two dead lovers, their blood mixing in the dirt and pine needles beneath them.

Arliss stared in shock. It was as though her heart had stopped and she was staring back at the world from a place just this side of death. A voice inside her head spoke to her. It told her to go to her mother. But she could not.

Her mother lay naked in death with Richard Neeley. The fact that she was naked and dead and lying in the arms of her dead lover so repelled the fifteen-year-old Arliss that when she regained some semblance of consciousness, she swung her horse around and galloped back across the stream, back in the same direction her father had gone as he fled the scene of his horrific crime.

Arliss looked up from her lap now to stare at her father, who stood, his arms hanging slack, staring at the floor in front of him. He looked as though he were in a daze.

"Neither one of us ever mentioned that day," Arliss said, brushing the tears from her cheeks. "All these years... we never said a word about it. It was a secret I helped you keep. Why?"

She shook her head. "I have no idea. Maybe because I was a coward. Maybe because I had no one to tell. Not even Johnny. I couldn't tell him what his father had done. I couldn't tell anyone. I couldn't even confront you with it... or leave here, which is what I should have done. Instead, I lived here with you, sharing your secret. Betraying the mother I loved. All I could do was hate you as you hated me for the secret you knew I was keeping, reminding you each day of the horrible thing you did.

"Finally, two years later, you found a way to get rid of me. You shipped me off to Roy Coates in return for his everlasting loyalty to you in town."

Arliss rose and walked over to stare down at her dead brother. She placed a hand on the side of Johnny's cold, pasty cheek.

"I'm as much to blame for his death as you are, Father. Johnny loved Mother more than either of us. His never knowing who killed her was sheer torture. All he ever knew was that she and Richard Neeley were found together, just as you left them. So he erupted with a violence he inherited from you. He gathered the roughest of your men and did exactly what you'd wanted him to do when you'd showed him their bodies, as if you were coming across them for the first time. He and those toughnuts rode over to Neeley's ranch, killed all of Neeley's men, and burned his headquarters to the ground."

Arliss turned to her father still staring at the floor. "You got Neeley's range in the bargain. I suppose you figured you deserved it." She looked at Johnny again. "Well, I hope you're proud of what you turned your son into. A man without a conscience. A frustrated bandit and killer out to murder the whole world as though he could kill his demons along with it. The joke was on him, though—wasn't it, Father? The real demon was you."

Stanley turned to Arliss. He blinked, staring at her dully. "Who killed my son? Tell me that and then leave. Get the fuck out of my house and don't you ever come back, you filthy bitch."

Arliss smiled. She wasn't sure why, but suddenly her father's words no longer hurt her. Her bitterness caused her to want to taunt him, to stick the knife in a little deeper and twist it. "That, dear Father, is something you're going to have to find out for your—"

"Gideon Hawk." The unexpected man's voice caused Arliss to jerk with a start.

She darted her gaze to the French doors and saw a man standing just outside them—a medium tall, deeply tanned man with a drooping mustache, floppy-brimmed canvas hat, corduroy breeches, and knee-high leather boots. He wore a black vest over a pinstriped shirt trimmed with a string tie. A pistol was thonged on his right leg, *pistolero*-style.

He stared into the parlor, slid his gaze between Arliss and her father, and then doffed his hat with an unctuous air.

He cleared his throat. "The man's name is Gideon Hawk, Mister Stanley."

Stanley scowled at the newcomer.

The man stepped into the room, holding his hat down low in front of him. "I'm John Donnan, Mister Stanley."

"I know who you are. Avril Donnan's brother."

"My brother died with your son, Mister Stanley. Hawk killed Dave Yonkers, as well."

"Hawk, you say?" Stanley's expression had turned incredulous.

"Gideon Hawk. Known by newspaper scribblers as 'the Rogue Lawman.'"

Donnan smiled with satisfaction. He had seedy, dark-brown eyes drawn up at the corners. Large, dark-brown freckles spotted his leathery cheeks. Arliss had seen him around town from time to time, sometimes with Johnny. She figured that, like most of those her brother had ridden with, he probably worked as little as possible.

Otherwise, he rode with Johnny, holding up stages, rustling cattle for outlaw syndicates, or getting involved in one small but bloody range war or another up north or down south.

There was always a squalid, seamy air about John Donnan. That air hung heavy on him today, here in the dilapidated parlor of the once regal Stanley house.

"The Rogue Lawman," Stanley said.

Arliss's heartbeat quickened anxiously as she studied her father, knowing what was to come.

"The Rogue Lawman," Stanley said again, musingly. "Why that handle?"

"The man was a deputy United States marshal over in Nebraska Territory. Then some gang led by 'Three Fingers' Ned Meade hanged his son. They was gettin' even for Hawk havin' run Meade's outlaw brother down. Same day as Hawk's boy's funeral, Hawk's wife hanged herself from a tree in their backyard."

Donnan apparently felt comfortable enough to have a seat on the same sofa on which Arliss had been sitting a few minutes earlier. He set his hat on his knee, leaned back, and placed his left arm on the sofa back, casually, as though he were an equal here.

He continued: "Some crooked prosecutor got Meade off, saved him from hangin'. Turned him loose. After that, Hawk went off his nut. He hunted the prosecutor down. Hanged him. Hunted the rest of Meade's gang down, killed 'em. Hunted Meade down. Hanged him. After that, he started wearin' his badge upside down. Now, he rides for his own brand of justice."

"Why did he kill my son?"

Arliss answered this one. "Johnny and Mister Donnan's brother and Yonkers were trying to hold up the Arkansas River Saloon."

Donnan said, "What I heard was Johnny tried to shake down Hawk. Apparently, Johnny didn't know the brand of man he was dealin' with."

Stanley turned to Arliss. "Where was your husband when all this was going on?"

"He was there." Arliss gave a sardonic snort. "He tried to arrest this Mister Hawk... and is now sporting about five broken ribs and a face that looks like freshly ground beef. He's in bed. Drunk."

"Where's Hawk?" her father asked, angrily.

Arliss said, "He left town."

At the same time, Donnan said, "He's still there." He glanced at Arliss, dubious. Switching his gaze back to Stanley, he said, "Johnny winged him. He'll likely be holed up till tomorrow mornin', at least. Last I heard, the doc sewed him up."

Stanley looked at Arliss. His eyes were hard, questioning, accusing. She held his gaze with a stern, accusing, mocking one of her own.

"What do you want, Mister Donnan?" he asked out of the side of his mouth.

Donnan gave a sheepish half-grin, hiking a shoulder. "Well... I know how much you value information on the doin's in town, Mister Stanley. Especially when it concerns you."

"Money?"

Donnan hiked his shoulder again, then smiled again, awkwardly.

Stanley turned to the liquor cabinet and refilled his goblet. He took a sip of the brandy and then walked over to the piano. He stood beside his daughter and stared down at his dead son glaring up from the Confederate flag.

"You want money for helping me better understand the circumstances of my boy's death." It wasn't a question.

Donnan's face darkened with a flush. He winced a little, shifting his head around on his shoulders, uncomfortably.

"I know you, Donnan. I know your family."

Donnan didn't say anything. Stanley threw back the entire goblet of brandy. Then he slammed the goblet down on the piano and swung around to face Donnan. He slid his revolver from his holster and clicked the hammer back.

"You're all Yankee trash. Always have been, always will be. And now you... you, common gutter trash... have the gall to ride out here in the aftermath of my boy's murder and seek to exchange information on the circumstances of his death for *money*!"

"No!" Donnan threw his hands up in terror. "Mister Stanley—hold on!"

"Yankee vermin!"

The gun slammed its report against Arliss's ears.

She jerked with a start, blinked, and stumbled back against the piano. She stared in shock at Donnan, who sagged back against the couch with a quarter-sized hole in the middle of his forehead. Arliss closed a hand over her mouth as though to stifle a scream that did not come. Befuddlement nearly overcame her. Her knees threatened to buckle.

She looked at her father, who grinned with satisfaction at Donnan, who now sat back against the couch, jerking wildly as he died, blood bubbling out of the hole in his forehead.

Stanley saw his daughter's horrified, incriminating gaze. He raised his pistol again, and aimed it at Arliss's head.

"Get out," he said through gritted teeth. "Go on back to your worthless husband. Tell him if he can't take care of the man who killed my boy, he's fired!"

Arliss stared at the maw of the revolver in her father's fist. It was only about three feet from her head. She was not surprised that she felt no fear at all. It had been a while now since she'd last cared if she lived or died. The way her life had gone since her father had killed her mother and Richard Neeley was like a nightmare she'd been living day by day, with no end in sight. Since it hadn't ended in the lake, it might as well end here as anywhere else.

Slowly, Arliss shook her head. "Who are you, Father? Do you know? Have you ever known?"

"I told you to get out."

"You started out well. Now, look around you." Arliss glanced at her dead brother atop the piano. She looked around the dusty room, cobwebs hanging like thin curtains from the ceiling corners, dead leaves on the rug. "All you had was ambition. That was all you ever had. You had no heart and no soul. Now, look what you've become. A lonely, raging, obsessed lunatic believing the world is closing in on him. Have you taken a good look at your men lately?"

Arliss arched a brow and looked at Donnan, who had now stopped quivering and was sagging against the couch as though napping.

"They're all the same trash as Mister Donnan there."

"I told you to get out," Stanley said. "I won't tell you again."

"You won't need to."

Arliss glanced once more at Johnny and then walked across the room and out the door.

She climbed into the undertakers' wagon and started down the trail to Cedar Bend. She hadn't ridden far when five riders overtook her from behind, and galloped past her. It was late in the afternoon. Copper sunlight winked off the guns the riders wore strapped around their waists or jutting from rifle scabbards.

They swept her with their lusty gazes as they passed, laughing. They galloped on ahead and disappeared.

Her father had sent them, Arliss knew. He'd sent them to Cedar Bend to avenge her brother.

Arliss shook the reins over the back of her horse. "Hy-yahh, boy. Hy-*yahhhh*!"

CHAPTER 10

A KNOCK SOUNDED ON THE DOOR OF ROOM NINE IN the Colorado Hotel.

Hawk was sitting in a chair by the window, hoping the glass of whiskey he was sipping would soon kill the pain in his arm. After the doctor had sewn and wrapped the wound, Hawk had taken a long nap. The pain had awakened him a half hour ago.

When the single knock had come, he'd been leaning forward in the chair, laying out a game of solitaire on the upholstered ottoman before him. Now he reached for one of his two holstered pistols, cocked it, and looked at the door, frowning.

"It's me," a young woman's voice said on the door's other side.

Hawk rose, wincing at the gnawing pain in his left arm. He wore only his balbriggan top, unbuttoned. He glanced at his shirt on the bed, then gave a wry chuff. She'd seen him in far less than his underwear. Keeping the cocked Russian in his right hand, because he wasn't one to take chances, he walked to the door, twisted the key in the lock, and turned the knob.

The young woman whose name Hawk had learned from the sawbones was Arliss Coates, the former Arliss Stanley, sister of dearly departed Johnny Stanley, stood in the hall, staring at him. Her cheeks were newly sunburned. Several locks of her dark-brown hair had pulled loose of the horse tail she'd gathered them in, and curled down against the sides of her face.

Her eyes were wide and bright.

She placed her hand on his chest, just above the open button V that exposed the inside slabs of his exposed pectorals. "You have to leave here!"

Hawk looked at her hand on his chest. She looked at it, too. Her cheeks flushed slightly. She removed her hand and then looked both ways along the hall. A half-dressed, middle-aged man with a bulbous paunch stood in a half-open doorway, holding a half-eaten sandwich. He stared at Arliss and Hawk dubiously, chewing.

Hawk stepped back into the room, drawing the door wide.

Arliss came in, and Hawk closed the door.

Arliss moved in close to stare up at him, her eyes anxious. "You have to leave here, Gideon. My father has sent men. They're in town. I just came from the undertakers' place, and I didn't see them on the street, but I know they're—"

She stopped when Hawk placed two fingers on her lips. "Drink?"

She frowned. More color rose in her cheeks. "What?"

Hawk walked to the dresser, grabbed his bottle, and held it up. "You look like you could use a drink."

She studied him incredulously. Then she looked at the bottle, and shrugged. "Why not?"

Hawk poured whiskey into a water glass on the dresser and took it over to her. "Ride a long way today, did you?"

She accepted the drink. "I took my brother home."

"Oh?"

Hawk sat back down in his chair and leaned forward, resting his elbows on his knees. "Have a seat."

Arliss strode past Hawk to stand beside the window flanking him. She slid the curtain back from the window and peered out, looking cautiously up and down the street. She turned to Hawk, sipped the whiskey, swallowed, and made a face.

When the rye had mellowed inside her, she said, "My father is a powerful man in these parts, Gideon. My brother cut a wide swath. Most folks let him cut it because my father usually made up for it, somehow."

"Is that a fact?"

"My brother once killed a shotgun guard on the local stagecoach. He was a young man with aging parents. My father built the guard's parents a new house and gave them a thousand dollars. Nothing more was said about the killing, and my brother was allowed to run free."

"Tidy."

"I am married to the man you beat the hell out of."

"The town marshal. I gathered that."

"My father forced me to marry Coates in return for Coates's loyalty to my father."

"Is that why you walked into the lake?"

Arliss didn't seem to know how to answer that. She gazed at her glass. She took another sip, glanced carefully out the window once more, then sat down near Hawk, on the end of the bed. "I don't think you understand. My father has fifteen, maybe twenty men. They're gunmen. My father believes someone's crowding him. He's sent five of those gunmen here. He can send more." She leaned forward, placing a hand on his knee. "You have to leave here, Gideon."

"I don't run, Arliss."

She studied him closely, her eyes probing his. After a time, a knowing smile shaped itself on her pretty lips, and she tapped the nail of her right index finger against the rim of her glass. "You don't care, do you? You don't care what happens. You don't care if you live or die."

Hawk shrugged and sipped his own rye.

"I heard what happened," Arliss said. "To your boy... your wife."

Hawk just stared back at her, stone-faced, the hand holding his drink resting on his right knee.

Finally, Arliss took another sip of her drink and then she rose and, holding the drink low in her left hand, walked over to him. She used her foot to slide the ottoman out of her path, and stood between his spread knees, crouching over him. She placed her right hand on his cheek. "All right, then. If anyone understands you, it's me. You've been warned. Tomorrow you'll likely be dead. Just know one thing. That night... by the lake..." She shook her head slowly. "I've never felt so alive."

Hawk took her hand in his, slid it to his mouth, and pressed his lips to it gently.

She drew a breath, tucked her bottom lip under her upper front teeth, then removed her hand from his and turned away. She walked to the door. She took too long opening it. By the time she started to slowly turn the knob, Hawk had crossed the room to her. He reached in front of her and turned the key in the lock, locking the door. She turned to face him.

Hawk sandwiched her face in his big hands and tipped her head back. She parted her lips for him, and he kissed her. She wrapped her arms around his neck and returned the kiss, hungrily, mashing her mouth against his and groaning deep in her throat.

Hawk felt his blood rise. He could feel Arliss's heart beating against his own. Her breasts swelled, pushing against his chest.

He kissed her with more and more passion, more and more hunger, before he drew his head back from hers, leaving her breathless and staring up at him, her eyes smoldering, lips parted. Hawk drew her over to the bed, gently pushed her down on it, then not so gently began removing her dress.

She let him do all the work himself, staring up at him, doe-eyed, her chest rising and falling sharply.

When he had her out of her clothes, she stood,

naked, and pushed him down on the bed. She pulled off his boots, tossing them away with dull thuds on the carpeted floor. She lay down beside him and, kissing him intermittently, playfully, unbuckled his cartridge belt. He pushed up on his elbows, arching his back, so she could slide the belt and the guns out from under him. Hawk tossed the guns up near the head of the bed, within reach if he needed them.

Even in the throes of carnal passion, Hawk was a cautious man...

Arliss kissed and nibbled his lips again for a time, raking her impassioned hands across his chest, kneading his pectorals through his longhandle top. She reached down and pressed her hand against his swollen crotch. Holding her mouth against his, she stretched her lips back from her teeth, giving a lusty smile, staring into his eyes, mesmerizing him.

She continued kissing him while her hands worked below his belly, unbuttoning his trousers. When she had them open, she scuttled down around his knees and grunted and groaned with the effort of sliding the trousers down his legs.

She tossed them away and then scuttled back up the long length of him and began sliding his long-handle top down his arms and chest. Her pale, tender breasts sloped toward his belly, jostling as she worked. Hawk reached out to fondle them, plying the burgeoning nipples.

She peeled the wash-worn cotton down his legs and over his feet and dropped the duds to the floor. She glanced up at him, tucked her hair behind one ear, smiled at him coquettishly, and took his throbbing member in one hand. Using her other hand to hold her hair back, she lowered her head to his crotch. She closed her lips over the head of his mast.

She slid her warm, wet lips down the length of him, teasing him with her tongue.

Hawk groaned as she plied him; he ground the backs of his heels and his fists into the bed.

When she'd toyed with him for almost longer than he could stand, she straddled him. He reached up and took her beautiful breasts in his hands, kneading them gently. She reached down below Hawk's belly, grabbed his mast, and lowered her bottom until he felt himself sliding inside her.

Deeper, deeper...

Hawk freed a held, heavy breath through his teeth.

"Oh, yes," Arliss whispered, breathless, her hair raking lightly across his chest. "Oh, yes." She straightened her back and squared her shoulders as she slowly rose and fell on her knees, closing her eyes, pressing her hands against his chest. "Oh, yes. Oh, god," she said. "I can die now... just any ole time..."

———

THEY MADE LOVE FOR MOST OF THE NIGHT.

Finally, they slept, Arliss resting her head on Hawk's chest.

Hawk rose before dawn. While Arliss continued to sleep deeply, curled into a ball in the middle of the bed, beneath the covers, he dressed, hooked his wounded arm in the sling the doctor had given him, left the hotel, and took a slow walk around the town, getting the lay of it, scouting for predators. The only other people he saw out and about at that early hour were a couple of shopkeepers either sweeping the boardwalks fronting their stores or splitting wood in the alleys behind them.

He bought a stone jug of coffee from a café, then returned to the hotel. The sleepy-eyed hotelier, Whitehall, was trimming the leaves of a potted palm in his lobby. Hawk asked the man to deliver a tub of hot water to his room, and the man delivered the tub a few minutes later, pushing through the door Hawk had left partway open. Hawk sat in the upholstered chair near the window, sipping a cup of coffee while Arliss continued to sleep deeply, the bedcovers rising and falling with her luxurious slumber.

Hawk pressed two fingers to his lips, shushing the hotelier, who turned to regard the sleeping woman incredulously, puffing his cheeks out and shuttling his incriminating gaze to Hawk. The rogue lawman grinned at the man, shrugging a shoulder.

Wagging his head disdainfully, the hotelier went out and came back several more times, pouring hot water into the tub. He came up a final time with a bucket of cold water, which he set down beside the steaming copper tub.

Arliss had roused while the hotel man had fetched the cold water. Now she lay with her head propped on her hand, her hair a lovely mess around her head and face. Her eyes glittering with sexual fulfillment, she smiled, blinking sleepily, at the hotelier, and said, "Mister Whitehall, have you ever felt as though you'd just died and gone to heaven?"

She thrust an arm and a clenched fist out, stretching.

Whitehall chuffed his disdain, puffed his cheeks out, and said, "What is your husband going to say about this?" He pointed at the rogue lawman.

"Mister Whitehall," Arliss said, resting her head on the heel of her hand again, "I just really couldn't give a good goddamn."

"I'm sure *he* could," Whitehall said, heading for the door.

A man's hoarse, bellowing cry rose from below. "*Arr-lissss?*"

Whitehall stopped and turned to the sleepy young woman in Hawk's bed. "Ah, Jesus—you're about to find out!"

"I reckon we will," Arliss said.

Coates bellowed his wife's name again so loudly that Hawk could feel the reverberation through the soles of his boots.

Whitehall went out, slammed the door, and stomped off down the hall. Two sets of boots pounded on the stairs. Coates was halfway through another bellowing yell when he cut himself off abruptly. Hawk could hear him and Whitehall talking on the stairs. Boots thudded again—angry, hammering thunder.

Coates came stomping down the hall.

"*Arliss?*"

She sat up in bed, holding the sheet over her

breasts. She slid her gaze to Hawk. He shrugged, then reached across his belly to slide his Russian .44 from the cross-draw holster on his left hip. He rested that elbow on the arm of his chair and casually hiked his right boot onto his left knee.

Arliss smiled. "In here, Roy!"

She let the sheet drop down below her breasts.

Coates's boots thundered in the hall. They stopped just outside the door.

Arliss's eyes brightened with expectation and excitement as they darted between Hawk and the door.

"Arliss, I know you're in there—you cheatin', fuckin' bitch!" With "bitch," Coates kicked in the door. The door hammered against the wall. As Coates bounded into the room, the door bounced off the wall and into Coates's right shoulder. He'd been carrying two pistols, but he dropped the one in his right hand with a yelp as he staggered to his left and dropped to a knee, groaning.

He tried to lift the pistol in his left hand, but it was as though the gun weighed twenty pounds. The man was obviously in pain. His face was badly swollen. Both eyes looked like pink eggs. His cheeks and lips were crusted with fresh scabs.

Hawk said, "No need to hurt yourself, Roy. The door was open."

Coates was panting. He stretched his lips back from his teeth as he cast his enraged, humiliated gaze from his bare-breasted wife sitting up in the bed before him, to the rogue lawman aiming his cocked .44

at him. Coates turned to Arliss again and bellowed, "You cheatin', filthy, back-alley bitch!"

Arliss laughed, showing her husband her love-chaffed breasts. "That's no way to talk, Roy." Now she hardened her voice, and, while her smile still quirked her lips, it had turned as brittle as January ice. "No way at all to talk to the back-alley bitch you raped on your kitchen table."

She looked at Hawk. "Meet the man who saved my life the other evening, Roy. I'd thought my life was over. I tried to drown myself in Pine Lake. He saved me." Her smile turned soft and sweet again, albeit it vaguely mocking, as well. She cupped her tender breasts in her hands. "In more ways than one."

Roy stared at her, panting as though he'd ridden a long way, spittle spraying through his gritted teeth. He started to turn his Remington toward her.

"Uh-uh, Roy," Hawk said aiming his own cocked Russian over his raised right knee, clicking back the hammer. "Drop the smoke wagon."

Coates turned to Hawk. "Fuck you!"

Hawk narrowed one eye as he aimed down the Russian's barrel.

Coates's eyes widened and brightened with fear. He depressed the Remy's hammer, leaned forward, and set the piece on the floor.

Hawk kept the Russian aimed at Coates's head. "Now, the badge."

"What?"

"The badge." Hawk wagged his gun barrel at the five-pointed star pinned to Coates's wool shirt. "Set it down beside the gun. I'm takin' over. I'm takin' your woman and your badge. Your entire town, matter of fact."

Coates just stared at him, his face a battered, puffy mask of speechless rage.

"Go ahead, Roy," Arliss said. "He's got your woman. Best give him your badge, too. Your badge and your wife or your life, Roy." She smiled.

Coates looked at her, silently snarling. He peered at Hawk staring down the barrel of his Russian at him. Coates gazed down at the star on his shirt. Cursing under his breath, he removed the badge and threw it down beside his gun.

It bounced and rolled and came to a rest on the floor near Hawk's chair.

"There, now," Hawk said. "That wasn't so hard —was it?"

"Who the fuck *are* you?"

Hawk just stared at him, expressionless.

"Take your leave, now, Roy," Arliss said. "We're going to take a bath."

Coates jerked an exasperated look at his wife. "Fuck you, Arliss!"

"No, Roy," Arliss said, smiling again. "Fuck you."

Coates rose awkwardly, grunting painfully, and staggered out of the room and down the stairs. Hawk got up, closed the door, and locked it.

He got undressed and crawled back into bed.

CHAPTER 11

HAWK AND ARLISS SPENT THE FIRST HALF OF THE morning in room nine of the Colorado Hotel, enjoying each other's company.

They bathed each other slowly, gently, intimately. Hawk had ridden the hard, bloody trail for a long time. It felt good down deep in his soul and soothing to his mind to spend some time with a woman. Making love to a woman. Getting to know a woman's mind as well as her body. He hadn't realized how much he'd missed that in the years since Linda's death.

When he'd finished bathing in the water Arliss herself had bathed in, she took her time drying him with a towel, lingering over his brawny nakedness, in her own supple, tender nudity, pausing occasionally to press her lips to the sundry scars marking him and that were a road map of his past several years on the hard-bitten frontier.

She'd removed the bandage on his left arm before

they'd bathed, and now she rewrapped it with fresh flannel greased with arnica.

His body clean and dry, Hawk dressed. He forewent the sling for his arm, as he had a feeling he'd need both hands free today. He stood at the window, staring into the street while he drew his shirt on over his balbriggan top, and buttoned the cuffs.

Behind him, Arliss dressed in front of the mirror mounted above the bureau. She spoke to his reflection.

"You know they're waiting for you out there," she said. "Especially now. After Roy..."

"Yeah," Hawk said, turning his head to thoroughly peruse the street. "But they're patient, I'll give them that. They're layin' low."

"There's five of them."

"That's what you said." Hawk reached behind him to pluck his vest off the bed; then, shrugging into it, he returned his gaze to the street bathed in golden morning sunlight. Dust rose from the churning wheels of supply wagons. "I reckon they're waiting for me to bring the fight to them." He nodded. "Yep. That's about the size of it."

Arliss turned to him, her expression one of tempered exasperation. "Why not leave, Gideon? Why stay here? They outnumber you. My father will not stop sending men until you are dead."

Hawk turned to her, reaching for his guns and shell belt hooked over the front bedpost. "Your father an' me got us an issue." He buckled the shell belt around his waist. "I'm gonna stay until the issue's settled."

Hawk donned his hat and walked to the door. "I reckon after what happened here, you'll be less than welcome at home. You'd best stay here until the matter's resolved."

Arliss sat on the edge of the bed, a hairbrush in her hands. "I have nowhere to go. But then, I've grown accustomed to that. I'll be here for you . . . if you need me."

Hawk smiled, pinched his hat brim to her, went out, and walked down the stairs. Whitehall stood on a chair in the lobby, setting a wall clock. He glowered as Hawk walked toward the front door.

As Hawk passed him, he asked, "You seen five Circle S riders in town?"

Whitehall nodded grimly.

"You know where they are now?"

"Arkansas River."

"Obliged."

"Don't mention it." Snootily, Whitehall said, turning his head to follow Hawk to the front door, "You ain't gonna be mentionin' much of *nothin'* ever again once you have a few drinks over there!"

Hawk went out and looked toward the north end of town. Five horses stood tethered to the hitchrack fronting the Arkansas River Saloon, lazily switching their tails. Two stood hipshot.

The sun was bright, and the heat was settling over this high-valley town. Woodsmoke remaining from breakfast fires wisped over the rooftops and false façades.

There wasn't much traffic on the street—only a

couple of farm wagons heading for Cruz's Grocery Store or the mercantile. A couple of elegantly attired middle-aged ladies were perusing the front windows of Mrs. Markham's Fineries for Women.

Hawk glanced around him quickly, making sure he wasn't about to step into an ambush, then crossed the street and headed north. The ladies in front of Mrs. Markham's eyed him dubiously as he passed on the canopied boardwalk, pinching his hat brim to each of them. They wrinkled their doughy noses at him. Obviously, word of the scandal at the hotel had made its way around town, as it would around any small town.

The notion amused Hawk. No one could have been less worried about scandal. At least, where it concerned him. As for Arliss, he didn't think she much cared what anyone around here thought of her anymore, either.

As he approached the saloon, he saw a man standing between the half-open batwings, staring Hawk's way. When Hawk met the man's incredulous gaze, the man's eyed widened in surprise. He pulled his head back into the saloon, and the doors fell into place.

As Hawk mounted the Arkansas's front stoop, he unsnapped the keeper thong from over his Russian's hammer and loosened the gun in its holster. He pushed through the batwings, stopped just beyond them, and cast his gaze quickly around the room.

The little barman with the ostentatious mustache —Joe Pevney—stood in place behind the bar. The riders from the Circle S sat at two separate tables to

Hawk's right. Two sat at a small, square table near the front windows. From there they had a good view of the street. The three others sat about halfway between the first two men and the bar.

The three had been playing cards, but none of the five were doing anything now except staring at Hawk.

They looked surprised to see him here, as though they'd thought they were going to have to root him out of some hole he was cowering in. They'd probably thought they were going to have to drag him kicking and screaming out of the hotel room he'd been sharing with Coates's wife.

Whatever they'd been thinking, they were definitely taken aback to see him here.

Hawk strode straight ahead to the bar. Pevney looked at the badge on Hawk's vest, and said with obvious disdain, "What're you doin' with Coates's star?"

"It's my star now." Hawk tossed his hat down on the bar. "Whiskey."

Pevney scowled as he popped the cork on a bottle and splashed whiskey into a shot glass. "What do you mean, it's your star now?"

"I mean this is my town now." Hawk was keeping an eye on the five Circle S riders in the back bar mirror.

They were shuttling their gazes from him to each other, shifting uncomfortably in their chairs. The leader of the toughnut group seemed to be a blue-eyed man with long, straight blond hair tumbling down from a brown bowler. The man's face, carpeted with a beard and mustache two shades lighter than his hair, was ugly as year-old sin. But his hair was as pretty as a girl's, though it had some seeds and trail dust in it.

The others looked toward this man as though inquiring for the go-ahead to start the dance...

The leader just sat back in his chair, staring dull-eyed at Hawk, his mouth forming a slash across the bottom third of his face.

"No better way to start the day than with a shot of whiskey," Hawk said, throwing back the entire shot, then slamming the glass back down on the bar top. He glanced at the five men glaring at him in stony silence. "Ain't that right?"

Hawk grinned and stared at the five Stanley riders, as though genuinely awaiting a response. When he didn't get one, he hardened his jaws, slid his hand across his belly to wrap his fingers around the butt of the Russian, and picked one of the five hired guns out of the group with his angry gaze. His voice thundered in the close confines: "I said there's no better way than to start the day with a shot of whiskey. Ain't that *right?*"

The man he had his eyes on jerked with a start, and said, "Yeah, yeah—that's right. Take it easy!"

Immediately, he flushed with embarrassment. The others looked at him, chuckling softly or sneering. All except the blond-headed gent in the bowler hat. He kept his hard blue eyes on Hawk.

"There," Hawk said with a nod. "That's better." He waved to Pevney. "I'll have one more. Figure it's a special occasion, since I'm starting a new job, an' all."

The ends of the barman's mustache twitched as he tilted the bottle over Hawk's glass. Hawk threw back the shot, slammed the glass down on the counter, and said, "All right—I'm off to my new job, I reckon." He smiled at Pevney. "Ain't you gonna wish me luck?"

Pevney slid his gaze to the silent Circle S riders, then raked out a sheepish, "Good luck."

"Thanks, Mister Pevney. I hope I won't disappoint you." Hawk donned his hat, winked, pinched his hat brim to the five Circle S riders, and strode out through the batwings.

———

OMAR YATES WAS THE BLOND LEADER OF THE FIVE men whom Stanley had sent to town to settle up with the man who had killed his son. Now Yates stared at the tall, broad-shouldered man in the black hat and black vest pushing through the batwings and stepping out onto the porch.

Through a front window, Yates watched Hawk descend the Arkansas's porch steps, swing sharply right, and head north along the main street. He was heading in the direction of Coates's office.

"Let's get after him!" said Phil Price, sitting to Yates's left.

"Oh, now you're ready to sic him," Yates said. "A minute ago I thought you were gonna piss your pants and soil your drawers."

The others snickered caustically.

"Nothin' better than a shot of whiskey to start the

day—ain't that right, Phil?" jeered Louis Sidner, a one-quarter Cheyenne gundog from Wyoming. He had one of his three pistols in his dark-brown hand on which he wore a turquoise ring. He was spinning the cylinder, enjoying the crispness of the whine.

"Fuck you fellas. He caught me off-guard." Price was enraged, humiliated. He slammed the heel of his hand onto the table he shared with Yates and said, "Come on, Yates—let's get after him!"

Yates leaned over the table and said slowly, softly, and with wide-eyed mockery, "We're gonna give him a minute, Phil. It's his first day on the job. It's only right we let him get situated."

"Fuck you, Yates!"

Yates's ugly face blossomed into a smile. "I know you been thinkin' about it, Phil. Just as long as you know that's all the further it's gonna go. You stay in your bunk. I'll stay in mine."

He winked.

The others had a good laugh at that. Price sat glaring at Yates, his ears as red as overcooked beets.

Yates rose and adjusted his brown bowler on his head. "All right, killer," he said to Price, throwing his long blond locks behind his shoulders. "Let's sic him."

Adjusting the set of his bowler hat, Yates sauntered toward the batwings. He glanced over at Joe Pevney, who was regarding the five gunmen from over the top of his bar, worrying one upswept wing of his mustache. "Leave our drinks where they are, apron. We'll be back for 'em."

He pushed out through the batwings. The others

followed him down the steps and up the street, heading north. The town marshal's office was a block and a half away. Men and women involved in the leisurely act of midweek commerce eyed the single-file striders skeptically from both sides of the street. A couple of doves were sunning themselves on the balcony of one of Cedar Bends two main-street pleasure parlors. Yates gave the girls a gentlemanly dip of his chin and touched his hat brim.

One of the girls, regarding him with the characteristically dull gaze of an overworked whore just waking up, blew cigarette smoke at him.

Yates slowed his pace when the jailhouse appeared thirty yards ahead. He stopped on the cross street. He looked at three of the men behind him, and said, "You fellas wait here. If you don't hear no shootin' inside of a minute, head to the back. He might try to skin out on us."

"All right, okay," said Sidner, holding his polished Bisley in his right hand and spinning the cylinder with his left. He was sweating, and his eager eyes were darting around in their sockets.

Yates looked at Price. "Come on, killer."

"Fuck you, Yates," Price said.

Curling a corner of his upper lip, Yates turned and continued up to the front of the jailhouse. He took a good hard look at the humble mud-brick place. Nothing looked amiss, though he couldn't see anything through the single dirty window left of the plank board door.

He pulled both of his Remington revolvers, clicked

the hammers back, and stepped onto the rotting boardwalk fronting the door and to the right side of which sat a hide-bottom chair, one leg propped on a flat stone. An uncorked bottle, likely belonging to Coates, a known tippler, stood beside the chair.

Yates stepped up to the door. Price stood to his right, both of his own pistols in his hands. Price had his chin down, nostrils flaring, lips pooched out—an angry bulldog eager for a reckoning. Yates gave a dry chuckle, then flipped the door latch and gave the door a light shove.

Hinges whined as the door fell back into the room.

The smell of sweat, whiskey, and pent-up air pushed against Yates, who looked into the shadows.

To his left was Coates's battered desk covered with what looked like common household trash—everything from yellowed papers to cigarette and cigar butts to corks to empty bottles and soiled drinking glasses. The only furnishings in the room were a potbelly stove, a rifle rack holding only one old Winchester on the far wall, a small table beside a dilapidated rocking chair with an Indian blanket draped over its back, and a cot with a rumpled army blanket and a sweat-stained pillow.

Yates moved into the room, glancing cautiously behind the door.

Nothing.

Price entering behind him, Yates walked farther into the room, as though the dingy, stinky shadows might reveal something with closer inspection. They did not.

"Must be back in the cellblock," Price said, standing by the stout cellblock door.

Yates grabbed a key ring off a peg in a ceiling support post, and tossed it to Price. Price tried several of the keys before finding the one that opened the cellblock door. He dropped the keys on the floor, shoved the door open, and stepped into the cellblock.

Yates followed Price down the narrow corridor. It was even darker in here than it had been in Coates's office, only two small, barred windows covered with a fine steel mesh allowing in natural light. There were two cells on each side of the block. All four were empty.

"Come out, come out, wherever you are," Price sang, his low voice echoing off the stone walls.

Following Price, Yates looked over the shorter man's left shoulder to see sunlight showing along the left side of the stout door at the end of the short corridor. The door wasn't latched.

"Must be out back," Yates said. "Hurry up, Price. Check it out."

Price glared over his shoulder at Yates. "Don't push me, damnit!"

Price walked up to the unlatched door. Yates could hear birds piping and weeds rustling in the breeze beyond it.

Price shoved the heavy door open with his right-hand gun barrel. Bright yellow sunlight angled through the narrow opening. Price shoved his left-hand gun through the opening. When he had half of his extended arm through the opening, the door slammed closed on Price's arm.

The doorway turned briefly dark. There was a wicked-sounding crack of breaking bone. Price howled miserably and dropped to a knee.

The door lurched open. A gun blasted. Price fell into the yard just beyond the door. Before Yates could wrap his mind around what had just occurred, half-blinded by the bright outside light being cast into the dark shadows around him, he saw a tall, hatted silhouette extend an arm at him

It was the last thing he saw before black wings engulfed him.

CHAPTER 12

THE BLAST WAS STILL ROCKETING AROUND INSIDE the cellblock as Yates staggered backward, his lifeless head wobbling on his shoulders. The hole from the .44-caliber round Hawk had just drilled through his forehead filled with dark-red blood.

Hawk lowered the smoking Russian, grabbed Yates by his shirt, and stepped to one side, twisting around as he thrust Yates out the open door and into the yard flanking the jailhouse. Hawk kicked the quivering legs of the first man he'd drilled out the door, then stepped back into the cellblock and closed the door.

Through the door he could hear men shouting and running toward him.

Hawk turned and strode down the cellblock. The cellblock door was partway open. Hawk stepped behind it just as light flooded the block from the rear. Someone had pulled open the back door.

Guns thundered.

Bullets cracked and whined and screeched around

the cellblock, clanking off bars. Several punched into the cellblock door behind which Hawk crouched, a grim smile twisting his mustached mouth.

"Die, you fucker!" one of the gunmen yelled beneath the near-deafening din.

One by one, the revolvers stopped blasting. Gun hammers clicked benignly onto firing pins.

Silence.

There was the metallic clicking of loading gates being opened and the tinny clatter of spent cartridges being dumped onto the stone floor.

Hawk's ears rang. Beneath the ringing, he heard a man say in a tight, apprehensive voice, "You think we got the son of a bitch?"

Hawk shoved the cellblock door away from him and stepped forward. "Nope."

Three man-shaped silhouettes stood in the sunlit doorway at the end of the cellblock, twenty feet away. All three were reloading. All three jerked their heads up and stiffened.

Hawk slid his Colt from its holster and then went to work with both the Colt and the Russian.

When he was done, all three man-shaped silhouettes had danced out the open back door. The only movement in the cellblock was the lazy buffeting of gun smoke touched with the lemon hues of the morning sun.

A boot scuff came faintly to Hawk's ears.

He jerked the cellblock door open. As he did, a gun flashed and roared from inside the jailhouse office. A bullet seared across Hawk's right cheek. He winced, raised his Russian, and fired three times at a shadow moving inside the office.

"Damn!"

There was a thud as the shooter, who'd fallen across Coates's desk, dropped to the floor. Hawk went in, kicked the fallen pistol away from the writhing figure of Roy Coates, and aimed the cocked Russian straight down at Coates's swollen face. One of Hawk's bullets had clipped the man's right arm. Another had drawn a blood-red line across the outside of his neck. There didn't appear to be any mortal wounds, but those two on top of the beating Hawk had given the former marshal earlier left him howling and kicking like a trapped wolf.

"Don't you die, you son of a bitch?" Coates railed up at Hawk.

"I'm beginnin' to ask myself the same question. Get up."

"I can't get up. I'm injured."

Hawk aimed down the Russian's barrel at Coates's head.

"Ah, shit," Coates said. "All right, all right, though where in the hell I got to go, I got no idea. My home is wrecked, thank you. And you have my badge."

"Shut up."

"Oh, fuck you!' That last was bellowed on the jailhouse's front boardwalk, for Hawk had shoved the former town marshal of Cedar Bend out the door.

Hawk pushed the man in the direction of the Arkansas River Saloon. As they slanted across the street, heading south, the undertaker, Charles

McCauley, stepped out of his furniture store. Wiping his hands on a rag, he gazed at Hawk.

"Got some more for me?" the undertaker asked, eyes brightly expectant.

Hawk jerked his head back to indicate Coates's office. "Behind the jailhouse."

McCauley winked and nodded. "Thanks!"

Hawk gave the slow-moving Coates another hard shove.

As he and the former town marshal continued toward the saloon, Hawk heard McCauley yell back into his store, "Buster, hitch up the mare!"

"Where the hell we goin'?" Coates asked, glancing over his shoulder at Hawk. "You mean to tell me you intend to buy me a drink? Thanks, but—"

Hawk pushed the man against one of the five horses standing at the hitchrack fronting the saloon. The horse gave a start, and Coates would have fallen if Hawk hadn't grabbed him again.

Joe Pevney came out of the saloon to stand before his sputtering batwings, both brows arched anxiously. The barman twisted an end of his mustache.

Hawk said, "Get up there."

"Huh?" Coates said, getting his feet settled beneath him again. "Get up where?"

Hawk glanced at the saddle. Coates followed his gaze, and his face crumpled with incredulity. "I can't ride!"

"Well, you're *gonna* ride." Hawk grabbed Coates's collar again, half-dragged and half-led him around to the left side of the horse while the four others whickered and sidestepped and pulled at their reins. "Get up there!"

"Where am I goin'?" Coates nearly screamed.

"Just let these Circle S mounts worry about that."

Hawk not so gently "helped" Coates onto the horse—a bright-eyed coyote dun that didn't particularly care for the strange maneuver nor the grunts and groans of the man being settled onto its back. When Hawk had Coates in the saddle, the rogue lawman cut the coiled *riata* hanging from over the horn into three two-foot lengths and used each of those lengths to tightly bind Coates's hands to his saddle horn and each foot to its corresponding stirrup.

"You're gonna kill me, you bastard!" Coates bellowed.

Folks had come out of the stores on both sides of the street to look on warily, muttering amongst themselves.

"When you get to the Stanley ranch," Hawk said, untying the horses from the hitchrack, "tell Stanley the local undertaker appreciates his business."

"My ribs are broken. Ridin's gonna drive one of 'em into a lung, and *you're gonna kill me!*"

Coates hadn't gotten that last out before Hawk fired both his pistols into the air over the horses.

The coyote dun and the other four mounts lunged off their rear hooves and broke into instant gallops, heading south toward their home in the mountains.

Coates's screams could be heard for nearly a whole five minutes before they finally dwindled to silence.

Hawk looked around. Townsfolk were staring at

him from various positions along the street, muttering amongst themselves.

"Chaos, eh?"

Hawk turned to Joe Pevney, still standing before the batwings, scowling at Hawk.

"Is that what you're all about, Mister Hawk? Yes, I know who you are. I overheard them five hammerheads talkin' in here earlier."

"All right," Hawk said. "You know. So what?"

"What are your intentions here? You've just run off our marshal after beating holy hell out of him. He might not have been much, but Coates was all we had. Lawmen are hard to find. Without the law around here, this place goes south real fast. Fills up with bad men of every stripe on the run from the law in other places. I see you're still wearing Coates's badge. Do you intend to stay here, to enforce our laws?"

Pevney shook his head. "I doubt that. A man like you can't stay in one place very long, though the argument is probably moot since Stanley won't rest until you're dead. That shouldn't take too long."

"I didn't start this fight, Pevney. Johnny Stanley did. He tried to rob you, you damn fool."

"A few years ago, when the Utes still ran amok in these parts, we said that we could afford to give up a cow or a horse or two to their braves, as long as that's all they took and didn't attack the town. Same with wolves. Allow them a calf or two in the spring, as long as they don't mess with the whole herd. Johnny Stanley was like that. We let him rob a saloon or a shop once or twice a year. Hell, it was sport for him.

His father settled the debt, anyway. At least, some-times he did."

"That's no way to run a town, Pevney. That's no way for a man to live his life—truckling to no-accounts like Johnny Stanley."

"Maybe you see things as black or white, Mister Hawk. That ain't no way for a man to live life, neither, because that ain't how life is."

"Johnny Stanley wasn't no Ute brave, Pevney. And he wasn't no wolf, either. He was a kid who hadn't been said no to nearly enough. I said no to him. As far as Coates goes, your marshal tried to arrest the wrong man." Hawk started walking toward the hotel, angling across the deserted street.

A hush had fallen over the town.

"What I'm tryin' to say, Mister Hawk," Pevney called to his back, his effeminate voice quaking a little with trepidation, "is thanks just the same, but we'll get along fine without your help!"

Hawk stopped and looked back at the barman. "No, you won't. Not if you don't stand up to bullies, Pevney. Even if they are the law. Even if they are rich and powerful. As soon as I'm gone, you can go back to hiding behind your counter and givin' away your money to men you're afraid of. Me? I'm gonna stay here and I'm gonna settle up with Stanley. Then and only then will I be on my way... if I'm not toe-down. Till then, you're stuck with me."

Hawk continued to the hotel. Whitehall was standing in the lobby, staring out the window. He gave

Hawk a constipated look and moved his lips as though he were trying to say something.

Hawk stopped, then looked at the man. "What's the matter, Mister Whitehall? Cat got your tongue?"

Hawk headed up the stairs. He knocked on his door, opened it, and stopped. Arliss stood before him. She wore her hat and the wool coat she'd worn when she'd first come to his room. She stood just inside the door, as though she'd been on the way out.

"Where are you going?" Hawk said.

"I'm going home to pack a few bags. A stage will pull through here tomorrow. I intend to be on it. I have an aunt, my mother's sister, in Denver."

Hawk studied her. Then he nodded. "That's probably wise."

Arliss walked up to him, placing a hand on his cheek. "Come with me, Gid?"

Hawk frowned at her, and placed his hand on hers, atop his cheek. He'd been about to say no, but he found himself hesitating, if only briefly. The hesitation surprised him. He'd never thought he'd ever settle down again. With anyone. The loss of his wife and son had left a hole in him that he'd thought no one else could ever fill.

Had he envisioned, however vaguely, Arliss filling it?

She seemed to sense that he had.

"Please," she urged. "We could travel far from here, start another life."

Hawk took her hand in his and pressed it to his

lips, kissing it. He shook his head. The faintest of grim smiles pulled at the corners of his mouth.

"It's too late."

"It's not, Gideon." Arliss implored him with her eyes as well as her words. "It's never too late. We could leave here... together. I know you're a wanted man, but you could change your name. We could marry, start a life together in a town where no one knows either of us."

"And do what?" Hawk said. "Buy a business? Run a mercantile? A livery barn? Maybe become farmers?"

"Or ranchers. I know the ranching business inside and out."

"Then that's what you should do," Hawk said. "Me?" He shook his head and pursed his lips.

Arliss swallowed, glancing at the floor between them. "If you stay, you'll die here. I don't want to be here to watch my father's men kill you. I can't." She looked up at him again. "We've known each other only a couple of days, but I feel like I know you almost as well as I know myself. You feel the way I feel, Gideon. We share a similar darkness. We can help each other."

"There's help for you, Arliss. There's no help for me. Outside of a gun, that is."

"Your guns will not bring your family back."

"I know that." Hawk frowned. "But... only half of me knows that. The other half thinks... that if I kill enough bastards who need killin'... they'll at least rest a little easier—Linda and Jubal."

Arliss shook her hair back from her eyes. Then she

rose up onto her toes and pressed her lips to Hawk's. "Goodbye, then, Gideon."

"Goodbye, Arliss."

"Oh, I forgot." She walked over to the dresser, plucked something off of it, and held her hand out to him. "I found this on the floor on your side of the bed. It must have fallen out of your coat pocket."

Hawk took the wooden horse out of her hand. It was the bucking black stallion that was the only thing he had left to remind him of his son. He ran his thumb across the deftly crafted mane and sleek neck. The horse looked real enough to gallop right out of Hawk's hand and into the next world.

"Thanks."

Arliss smiled, stepped around him, and moved out into the hall. She stopped and glanced back over her shoulder. "If you reconsider, I'll be in Roy's house till nine tomorrow morning. That's when the stage pulls out."

"All right."

"Goodbye."

"Goodbye, Arliss."

And then she was gone, and Hawk felt a sharp stab of the loneliness he'd thought he'd become inured to.

CHAPTER 13

A RAUCOUS COUGHING/STRANGLING SOUND WOKE Mortimer Stanley out of a dead sleep in his chair on the porch of his once impressive ranch house.

The rancher jerked his head up off his shoulder and kicked out with both mule-eared boots, gasping. He saw a crow staring at him through pellet-sized black eyes from its perch on the porch rail before him.

"You blasted vermin!" Stanley tried to shout, but the words came out sounding more like the bird's own raspy caw. "I was dead asleep, an'... an' you woke me... like to give me a heart stroke!" He leaned forward and coughed. "Mangy critter. Winged viper..."

Stanley frowned as he studied the bird, almost as large as some eagles he'd seen, and black as the blackest night. The rancher canted his head to one side, narrowing one eye suspiciously. "Why do you pester me so, crow?"

He'd awakened that morning to find the crow perched atop his son, Johnny, who still lay sprawled belly up on Stanley's piano. (Mortimer intended to get his son in the ground soon, but at the moment he just couldn't part with the child. The grave just seemed so *final...*) The wretched, carrion-eating bird had been dipping its beak into the corner of Johnny's right eye, pulling up some clear, jelly-like substance. Horrified, Stanley had run to fetch his double-barrel shotgun.

By the time the rancher had returned to the parlor with his gun in hand, the crow was gone.

That wasn't the first time the crow had appeared to Stanley. It had been showing up for weeks, intermittently. Lately, those visits had been growing more and more frequent. It was as though the crow was a warlock sent by some hoodoo witch to haunt him and taunt him for his past transgressions.

A few days back, he'd been dreaming of his beloved Caroline—yes, he'd loved his beautiful wife despite their wretched daughter having accused him of being incapable of love!—and just after she'd come to him in a diaphanous gown that had billowed out around her like angel's wings, only to have her turn to dust in his embrace, he'd awakened to find the crow perched atop his bureau.

The bird had been staring at him as it studied him now, its little, black, pebbly eyes strangely opaque but also accusing, jeering.

"What do you want with me?" Stanley asked the bird through gritted teeth. "Out with it, bird! Cat got your tongue?" He gave a weak chuckle at that. "What is it? Who sent you here?"

The bird gave another caw that resounded

wickedly inside Stanley's tender, whiskey-sodden brain, then lifted one wing and probed with its stiletto-like beak for mites.

The sound of drumming hoofbeats drew Stanley's attention beyond the bird and down the long hill toward the bunkhouse and other outlying ranch buildings and corrals. Several horses were just then galloping into the yard.

When Stanley had fallen asleep in his chair, he'd been bathed in the warm, lemony hues of a midafternoon sun. But now only a coppery, late-afternoon light remained, and cool shadows were descending from the high peaks that hemmed in Stanley's once-vibrant mountain stronghold.

The dust the horses pulled into the yard glistened like newly minted pennies. The horses ran up to the stable, where the barn shadow all but concealed them from the rancher's probing gaze. Before they'd disappeared, however, he'd thought he'd seen something on the back of one of the mounts.

Stanley scowled down the hill, puzzled, his alcohol-drenched brain working sluggishly, but a dull apprehension began to wrap itself around him like a cold, wet cape.

"Five horses," he muttered to himself, running his thumb and index finger down his jaw. "Five... horses... "

Then it nudged him like a poke from a sharp stick.

He'd sent five men to town earlier that day. At least, he'd thought it was that day. Wasn't it? Yes, he was sure it was...

The wet cape drawing tighter about his already-chilled frame, Stanley rose heavily from his hide-bottom chair and ambled to the porch rail. The crow stretched its neck at him, gave two more jeering admonishments, then lifted its wings, rose from the rail, twisted around in the air, and wheeled off down the hill and over the bunkhouse where the mountain shadows, nearly as dark as the bird itself, consumed it.

Stanley saw his men begin to gather around the five horses. He could hear them muttering incredulously amongst themselves. Sweat glistened silver on the horses' withers.

The man whom Stanley considered his foreman—a big, sullen but capable three-quarter Indian named Wilfred Red Wolf—turned toward Stanley. The rancher could always pick Red Wolf out of his small crowd of ranch hands down there. Red Wolf was a six-foot-six mountain of a man who wore a low-crowned, snuff-brown sombrero ornamented with the teeth of several U.S. soldiers his father had killed when he'd fought with Custer at the Greasy Grass.

He wore a long bull-hide duster and two cartridge bandoliers around his broad waist. Now in the shadows around the horses, the cartridges flashed like sequins on a debutante's ball gown.

Stanley threw his arm up and beckoned.

He watched the shadowy mass of men and horses mill in the salmon-touched copper light until one horse and Red Wolf separated from the crowd. Standing nearly as tall as the horse's head, Red Wolf led the horse up the hill in his slow, dogged, trudging way. As the foreman and the horse came to within fifty yards of the house, into the dull saffron sunlight still bathing the hill, Stanley could see a man sat astraddle the mount.

Actually, he hung half down the right side of the beast.

Red Wolf stopped the horse in the yard. The big foreman stared in silence at Stanley, who was now walking carefully down the veranda steps. He crossed the small yard and pushed through the arched trellis tangled with dead vines and looked from the broad, expressionless face of Red Wolf to the man hanging from the horse.

"What the hell...?" Stanley said.

He walked over to stare down at Roy Coates, whose feet were tied to his stirrups. Coates's bound wrists were tied to his saddle horn. He was slumped against the horse's right wither. He didn't appear to be conscious. Maybe not even alive. Stanley couldn't tell if he was breathing.

"Go around there and cut his foot out of that stirrup, Red Wolf."

When the big Indian foreman walked to the other side of the horse, Stanley used his own folding Barlow knife to cut Coates's right boot free of its stirrup. Together, he and Red Wolf cut the ropes binding the town marshal's hands to the saddle horn. When the final strands broke, Stanley stepped back quickly as Coates tumbled out of the saddle to hit the ground with a dull thud and a faint groan.

He lay on his side, stretching his lips back from his blood-frothed teeth.

Stanley kicked the man onto his back.

"What in tarnation...?"

Coates's face was a bloated mess. It looked like a cut of meat that had been left outside to rot in the sun and be nibbled on by predators. The marshal opened his eyes, and blinked.

"Coates?" Stanley said. "You worthless piece of shit."

Coates stared up at him for a time. Then Stanley wasn't sure if it was a pain spasm or a slight grin that tugged at the man's battered, swollen lips, but he had a feeling it was a grin. Coates swallowed, tipping his head back a little. It was a gesture for Stanley to bend an ear.

The rancher got down on one knee and lowered his head to within a foot of the marshal's mouth. "What is it? Get on with it. You don't got much longer on this side of the sod, Roy."

Coates opened his mouth, but spoke too softly and gravelly for Stanley to understand.

"What? Speak up, goddamnit," the rancher intoned. "I can't hear you!"

Coates made some more sounds. Stanley cursed and lowered his ear to within six inches of the man's mouth.

Coates raked raspily out: "She's fuckin' him. Arliss is..."

Stanley jerked his head with a start, turning to glare down at the marshal smiling up at him. Coates blinked slowly. A little more loudly, he said, "He said to tell ya... you're makin' McCauley a happy man."

"Oh, he did, did he?" Stanley said, pushing with a grunt off one knee, straightening. "Roy, you're a worthless mound of dog dung—you know that?"

Coates only smiled up at him, in a dreamy near-death state.

Stanley pulled his pistol, clicked back the hammer, aimed at Coates's head, and blasted a hole through the man's left temple. With the pistol's roar, the horse whickered loudly, leaped off all four hooves, turned, and galloped off down the hill toward the corral.

Stanley clicked his Colt's hammer back and shot the town marshal again. Coates's head turned sharply, as though he were obstinately disagreeing with Stanley's assessment of things. More frothy blood sputtered on his lips, like hot butter in a skillet, and then he gave a couple of feeble death jerks and lay still.

Stanley turned to Red Wolf standing beside him. "Send every last man I got. Tell them if they don't kill that man in town... that Gideon Hawk, the rogue lawman character... to not bother comin' back here. They will not be given their final paychecks."

Red Wolf gave a single, resolute nod, then started retracing his steps back down the hill.

"Hey?"

The foreman stopped, then glanced back over his shoulder at Stanley.

"You stay here. In case he gets around 'em."

Red Wolf gave that purposeful nod again, then continued down the hill.

———

HAWK ROSE THE NEXT MORNING FEELING refreshed. He was surprised to find that his arm, which had been aching devilishly since Coates had shot him, no longer hurt. He'd slept deeply. He didn't think he'd even been stirred by dreams, which was odd. Ever since he'd laid his family to rest, his slumber had been haunted.

He sat on the edge of the bed, staring into the misty shadows of the early dawn, blinking, wondering why he felt so light and awake and energetic, his mind already sharp.

So alive.

Then, he knew. There was a good chance that by the end of this morning, he would be joining his flower, his beloved Linda and that rascal son of his, Jubal. Joining them in heaven, if the stories were true. Or in the earth, if they were not. Wherever he ended up, he was certain to join his wife and son.

He pushed up from the bed, humming an old song he and Jubal used to sing when they'd walked out to the creek with their fishing poles. Drawing only a blanket around his shoulders, and not bothering with his boots, he walked downstairs in his stockings, found Whitehall sweeping dust and tumbleweeds off his veranda, and ordered a bath.

"Never seen a man take so many damn baths!" the hotelier complained, blowing smoke out around the quirley dangling from between his lips.

"It's a special day, Whitehall," Hawk said, and turned away.

"Special, huh? Yeah, I reckon it's special," the hotelier groused to Hawk's retreating back. "It's the day you're gonna die, unless you pull foot out of here while you still can!"

Hawk merely threw an arm up in acknowledgment as well as in dismissal of the man's advice. Hawk sat smoking a stogie he'd been saving for a special occasion, in the upholstered chair by the window, when Whitehall came up with two buckets of steaming water. The hotelier looked at the rogue lawman incredulously, shaking his head, as he poured the water into the tub.

After he'd added the last bucket of hot water and set a bucket of cold down next to the tub, Whitehall scowled at Hawk, breathing hard, fists on his broad hips. "I don't understand you. You must have something wrong in your head. Why don't you just ride out away from here?"

"My reasons are none of your business, Whitehall."

"All right, all right." Whitehall turned to the door. When he got to it, he stopped and turned half around to regard Hawk once more. "It's just that I hate to see a decent man die so needlessly. Whatever they say about you, and despite your dalliance with Miss Arliss, you do seem decent. You could make a good mark if you put your mind to it."

Hawk gazed back at him flatly, casually puffing his cigar.

"The problem with you," Whitehall said, pointing an accusing finger, "is you make too many enemies."

Hawk pulled the fat cigar out of his mouth and

blew smoke rings in the air before him. "Thanks for the water."

"All right, all right," Whitehall repeated, throwing his arms into the air.

He left the room and drew the door closed behind him.

Hawk rose, tossed away his blanket, stripped out of his balbriggans, and stepped into the bath. He sat in the steaming tub for a long time, smoking, leaning back with a dreamy smile on his rough-hewn but handsome face, studying the ceiling. Finally, he lathered himself from head to toe, scrubbed himself raw, then climbed out of the tub, toweled off, and dressed slowly, carefully, taking special care with his appearance.

After all, it might be the last time he dressed himself. Not that he needed to look good for the undertaker, but he'd been anticipating this day for a long time. It felt good and right to heed details this day. After all, it was a special day indeed.

Hawk combed his hair in front of the mirror above the bureau, and raked a hand across his jaws. He frowned at the stubble pricking his palm. He needed a shave.

To that end, he finished dressing, put on his hat, carefully adjusting the angle in the mirror, then grabbed his rifle, and left the room. He looked around the street. Seeing no sign of Stanley's men—there would likely be more today than yesterday—he headed over to Albright's Barbershop. He had to wait a few minutes for an old-timer to get a trim, then stepped up into the chair.

"Shave," he told the barber, Alvin Albright—a thick-waisted, bald man with swept-back brown muttonchops and a mustache nearly as wild as Joe Pevney's.

"Hair's gettin' a little long," Albright said to Hawk in his mirror, arching both brows and giving a salesman's roguish, slightly sheepish grin. "You're a good two inches over the collar."

"I am at that," Hawk said, canting his head this way and that in the mirror. "Take a little off the back forty, will you? And let's give my ears a little sun."

"Why not?"

Albright chuckled as he drew the pinstriped cape around Hawk's shoulders and snapped the paper collar into place around his neck.

"Funny," the barber mused, as he combed and snipped at the back of Hawk's head.

"What's funny?" Hawk asked, holding his chin down and regarding the man in the mirror.

"Mort Stanley is likely emptying out his bunkhouse right now, sendin' all hands this way to take you down. And you..." Albright gave his head a single, puzzled wag. "You don't seem one bit het up about it, when most men would be long gone or pissin' down their legs." He frowned at Hawk in the mirror. "You actually think you can *take* all them?"

He stopped cutting for a moment.

Hawk gave the barber's reflection a patient look in

the mirror. "If you don't mind, Albright, I'd rather you worked more and talked less."

"All right, all right," the barber said, his clippers starting to clip away again. "Just curious, is all."

"This town has a bad case of that."

The clippers stopped clicking again when the thunder of many hooves rose and a man's voice sounded, bellowing stridently.

Automatically, Hawk tensed in the chair. He was about to rise and head over to where his Henry leaned against the papered wall, when Albright, who'd gone over to one of the front windows to peer out, said, "The mornin' stage from Carthage."

Hawk got out of the chair and stepped through the door Albright had propped open with a rock. He looked up the street to his left, where the Wells Fargo office sat across from the town marshal's office. Hawk knew a moment's prickling regret when he saw Arliss standing there in a cream traveling suit and matching plumed picture hat. Several smaller bags stood near her feet on the boardwalk fronting the office, abutting a large steamer trunk.

Arliss stood gazing up at the station while two passengers climbed out of the carriage and two hostlers hurried up from a broad break between buildings, leading a fresh team from the relay barn. Arliss dipped her chin suddenly and then, as though she'd sensed Hawk's stare, turned her head slightly toward him.

Her eyes met his. She held his gaze for a moment

with an oblique one of her own. Then she turned her mouth corners down and looked away.

"Mrs. Coates," the barber said. "She must be pullin' foot... now that her husband ain't in such good health no more."

Hawk turned to Albright, whose face flushed sheepishly. Then the barber slid his eyes beyond Hawk to the stage again, and said in a philosophical tone, "I don't know what it is, but I've always admired to see the stage come and go. You know—bringin' people in, movin' 'em out. I guess it talks to my own wanderlust."

Hawk moved back into the shop and retook his perch in the chair.

The barber followed him in and went back to work, the clippers clipping away.

Fifteen minutes later, when Albright had finished Hawk's hair trim and was half done with his shave, Hawk heard a bellowing cry. He started to tense again automatically. But then there was the pop of a black-snake over the backs of the fresh stage team.

Hooves rumbled. A horse whinnied shrilly, indignantly.

Hawk shoved the barber's hand away from his face and tripped the wooden lever that righted the chair, so he sat level with the front window.

He peered out as the team whipped into view, in a full gallop, heads down, ears pinned back. The coach jounced along behind. Arliss sat on the coach's near side, facing forward. She was looking out the window toward Hawk. She and the coach passed in a jostling blur, but just before she was gone, she lifted her right, white-gloved hand in a parting wave.

Albright gave a crude snort.

Hawk glanced at him. Again, the barber flushed, sheepish.

Hawk tripped the lever again, and the chair fell back.

It just so happened that at the same moment Albright was scraping the last of the rogue lawman's beard from his right cheek, Hawk again heard the thundering drum of many hooves. He did not tense this time as he'd tensed before. He was ready for them now, having expected them for the past couple of hours.

The drumming grew louder and louder until it was joined by the jangle of bridle chains and the squawking of leather tack.

Hawk winced when Albright's right hand, which had been rock steady until now, quivered slightly, and the razor pricked him.

"Oh!" Albright grunted, lifting the blade to see the snowy, rippled mound of lather touched with dark-red blood.

"That's all right." Hawk shoved the man's hand aside with his arm, then grabbed the towel off the barber's shoulder, and swabbed it across his face. "You did good, Albright."

"Ah, shit," the barber said, scowling at the nick on Hawk's cheek. "Sorry about that. I pride myself on—"

"Think nothing of it."

Hawk patted his cheek until he stopped seeing

blood on the towel. Then he tossed the towel back over the barber's shoulder and smiled. "See there? It's already clotted."

The drumming of horse hooves had stopped. It was followed by an eerie silence. Wisps of sunlit dust moved along the street fronting the barbershop, drifting there from the south.

The barber drew a deep breath and then wiped the razor on the towel.

Hawk rose from the chair, ripped off the cape, and tossed it over a chair arm. He reached into a pocket of his whipcord trousers. "How much?"

"On the house," Albright said, waving a hand.

"Normally I'd appreciate that," Hawk said. "But under the circumstances..." He stuffed a half-eagle coin into the barber's shirt pocket. "McCauley's made enough money off of me."

He gave the barber a wink, then grabbed his hat from a peg and picked up his rifle.

Outside, in the direction of the hotel, a man shouted, "Hawk!"

Albright gasped and jerked a look out into the street. "That's them. They're here for you."

"What?" Hawk said, adjusting the angle of his hat. "You think they wouldn't come?"

CHAPTER 14

HAWK SHOULDERED HIS RIFLE AND STEPPED OUT through the door. Stopping on the boardwalk fronting the shop, he looked to his right up the broad main street. The hotel stood a block and a half away. A dozen or so horseback riders sat in front of it, staring toward the hotel.

One of them cupped his hands around his mouth and shouted, "Hawk! Gideon Hawk! Mortimer Stanley's got a bone to pick with you, Hawk!"

Hawk smiled. He started to step into the street but stopped when he saw two people staring at him from an alley mouth between a ladies' hat shop and a feed store. Hawk's heart hiccupped, then quickened.

His wife and son, Linda and Jubal, stood there in their Sunday finest, smiling at him expectantly. Linda's blond hair curled onto her shoulders. She held young Jubal's hand as he stood beside her in his knickers and long, wool socks. They each appeared just the way they had when Hawk had last seen them, before he'd laid them to rest only one day apart.

Hawk's eyes brightened beneath the broad brim of his black hat. "Soon," he whispered. "Soon..."

Linda's smile broadened, as did Jubal's. Then they turned and walked off down the break between buildings, and disappeared.

Hawk felt a sob well up in his throat. His eyes stung.

"Hey!"

Hawk glanced at the hotel. One of the Stanley riders was pointing toward Hawk. The others swung their heads toward him now. Hawk swallowed the knot in his throat, reached into his right vest pocket, and pulled out Jubal's horse. He held it before him, smiling down at it, then lifted it to his lips and kissed it.

"Soon, Jube," he whispered to the carving. "Soon."

In the periphery of his vision, he could see the Stanley men dismounting and shucking their rifles from saddle scabbards. Hawk replaced the carving in his pocket, took the Henry in his right hand, and stepped down off the boardwalk. He rested the repeater on his shoulder as he walked into the street.

The Stanley riders were all walking toward him now in a steadily loosening clump, spreading out around and behind one man—the apparent leader of the pack. He was maybe thirty—tan and pockmarked and with a thick mustache that angled down wide of his chin. He wore three pistols, and he had a

Winchester carbine in both gloved hands. A big Bowie jutted from his right boot well.

He stopped about forty yards from Hawk, the morning breeze tugging at the old, dark-blue, sun-faded army jacket he wore over a buckskin shirt. The eyes beneath his hat brim were cornflower blue. They were the eyes of a pretty girl set in the deep sockets of a Missouri outlaw's sneering face.

T. J. "Cord" Jessup.

The name popped off some wanted dodger and into Hawk's head. Due to his lawman's training, he had a memory for names he'd spied on wanted circulars. He thought he could probably fit names to the raggedy-heeled, unshaven, hard-eyed lot flanking Jessup as well, if he wanted to. But there was no point. He'd take down a few of the twelve facing him now—as many as he could before the law of averages did him in—and call it a life.

Hawk faced the bunch, opening and closing his hand around the neck of the Henry riding his shoulder.

"You Hawk?" Jessup called.

"That's right."

Jessup blinked, lifting his chin slightly, with acknowledgment. He canted his head to one side and half-smiled as he said, "Our boss, Mister Mortimer Stanley, would like a word."

A couple of the men around him chuckled at that.

"Why don't you just relay a message for me?" Hawk said.

"What message is that?"

Hawk kept his flinty, jade gaze on Jessup's corn-flower blues for about seven seconds. Jessup's eyes began to flicker a little with acknowledgment of Hawk's intentions. They darted full wide as Hawk jerked the Henry off his shoulder, thumbed the hammer back as he snapped the stock's brass plate to his shoulder, aimed down the barrel, situating the sites on Jessup's chest, and fired.

Jessup had timed his own move a quarter-second too slow.

Just as he leveled his own rifle on Hawk, the rogue lawman's bullet shattered his breastbone and shredded his heart, punching him backward, tripping over his heels and triggering his rifle into the street before him. He didn't scream, but only hardened his jaws and blinked his wide eyes in exasperation at his mistake— believing that he was the one calling the shots, that he was the one who would have the honors of starting the dance.

Hawk dropped two more but then the lead started flying his way, screeching through the air around him. One seared a hot line across the side of his left knee. He thought he could drop one, maybe two more before they...

But then one fell that Hawk hadn't shot.

Another screamed and twisted around, then, blood oozing from his lower left side, cast an enraged glare to Hawk's right, where the little barman from the Arkansas River Saloon, Joe Pevney, was down on a knee behind a rain barrel, triggering two pistols over the barrel and into the jostling crowd of Stanley shooters.

Before the man Pevney had shot could return fire at him, Pevney triggered one of his two mismatched revolvers once more, and the wounded man bought another round—this one to his forehead.

Hawk had been distracted only one fleeting second by Pevney's unexpected display. Now he dropped to one knee and continued firing, accounting for two more screaming, dancing Stanley riders but not the one he just now saw drop to the street clutching his right knee. Grimacing and clamping a hand over his bloody leg, the Stanley rider turned to Hawk's left, shouting, "Whitehall, what the fuck you think you're doin', you son of a bitch?"

Hawk glanced over to where the hotelier, Chester Whitehall, wearing a floppy-brimmed canvas hat and a holstered pistol, was triggering an old Sharps carbine at the Stanley riders, wincing and flinching as return fire drilled bullets into the feed store behind him.

Hawk racked another round into the Henry's action, and sited down the barrel.

There were only three or four riders left standing, dancing around and dodging bullets while looking exasperated and trying to trigger their own rifles. A Stanley man was down on one knee, tossing his rifle away and reaching for the two pistols on his hips. Before Hawk could shoot him, either Pevney or Whitehall took the honors. The man slumped backward, dropping one pistol to clamp his hand over the blood-geysering hole in his neck.

Hawk swung his Henry's barrel to his right as one of the few still-kicking Stanley riders turned to run toward the right side of the street, loudly bellowing curses. Hawk shot him between his shoulder blades and the man flew forward off his boots, landing on a boardwalk and then colliding violently against the front wall of the Miller Family Drug Emporium.

Another man ran off the street's left side, kicked open the door of a shoe store, and disappeared inside.

Whitehall cackled a wild laugh and, clutching his own bloody left leg, yelled, "Look at him run!" He laughed again. "I ain't had that much fun since the last Ute attack damn near ten years ago!"

Hawk looked at the Stanley men. They were all down. Most were unmoving. Two were moaning and writhing.

Hawk turned to Whitehall and said, "What the hell are you doin'?"

"You was right," Pevney said, rising from behind the barrel on the opposite side of the street from Whitehall. "It was time we took town matters into our own hands—since it is *our town*, an' all!"

"And since you're only one man against a whole horde," Whitehall said, grinning, proud of himself despite the bloody leg. "Hell, me and Joe fought Injuns together before we settled down here. I reckon we forgot we got it in us to hold the wolves at bay—eh, Joe?"

"You got it, Ches!" Pevney said, grinning and twisting an end of his mustache. "Did you see how I gutshot that consarned Donny Houston. There he is there—the pile of beef in the red shirt!"

"Good one, Joe!"

There was the tinkle of breaking glass. A gun popped from the direction of the shoe store. The bullet plunked into the rain barrel near Pevney.

Hawk shouted, "Get down, you crazy bastards!"

A girl's scream followed the pistol's blast out of the shoe store.

"Oh, no," said Whitehall, hunkered behind a square-hewn awning support post. "That's Janey Ryan. She's in the shoe shop alone today, as her pop took sick over the weekend!"

"Stay here and keep your heads down." Hawk raked a round into the Henry's action, then jogged through a narrow alley on the street's left side. At the end of the alley, he turned to his right and ran behind several buildings until he came to the rear of the shoe shop.

He pulled the door open and found himself behind the shop's rear business counter, staring at shelves of displayed or boxed shoes extending beyond, toward the front of the store, which he couldn't see from his vantage. A schoolbook lay open on the counter near Hawk, a pencil resting in the crease between pages, a lined note tablet peeking out from under the book, above a wood stool over which was draped a knitted blue sweater.

From somewhere near the front of the store, a girl's frightened, quavering voice said, "Pl-please don't hurt me. Please... please, don't hurt me!" She broke down in sobs.

"Shut up, goddamnit!" a man voice thundered. "I told you to shut up or I'd drill a hole through your purty head!"

Hawk moved into the store and stepped through a break in the counter. From the front of the shop came the clanging rattle of a cowbell. The girl continued sobbing. Hawk moved to his left in front of the counter and stopped to gaze up a dark aisle toward the front.

The Stanley rider was sidestepping through the open front door, holding a young, long-legged girl in a checked gingham dress and with dark-blond hair in front of him. He pressed the barrel of a cocked, long-barreled revolver to the girl's right temple. The girl's lips were fluttering as she sobbed.

Hawk raised his rifle and aimed up the aisle, but then the Stanley rider pushed on outside, and the door closed behind him and the girl, obscuring Hawk's shot. When the Stanley man and the girl had dropped down the shop's front porch steps, Hawk hurried to the front of the store and stared through the door's window.

The Stanley rider—tall and dark and with a broad, fleshy face carpeted in ratty patches of a cinnamon beard—stepped out into the street, shoving the girl ahead of his with his body, keeping the revolver's barrel pressed to her head. He was staring up the deserted street to Hawk's right.

"Where are you, Hawk?" the man shouted. "You

come out where's I can see you! I'm gonna kill this girl less'n you don't give me free passage back to my hoss! Understand?"

He looked around, swinging his head from left to right as he continued to shuffle up the street near where the other Stanley men lay dead. "You hear me, Hawk?" he shouted shrilly, his voice echoing off the false façades around him. "You come out where I can see you, or I *will* drill a bullet through this girl's *head*!"

Hawk took one step back from the door. He pressed his Henry's rear butt plate against his shoulder, and aimed through the door's window, clicking the hammer back with his thumb. He lined up the beads on the Stanley rider's head and was about to squeeze the trigger when the man turned abruptly, half-facing Hawk. Now the girl's head obscured the Stanley man's.

Hawk pulled his head away from his rifle, scowling.

"Hawk, goddamn you!" the Stanley rider shouted. "This ain't no game, now. If you don't show yourself in three seconds, I'm gonna blow this purty li'l gal's brains out!"

"No!" the girl sobbed, her face a mask of terror.

"One..." the Henry rider shouted, turning slowly back to stare up toward where Hawk had faced the gang.

"Two..."

The rider pressed his pistol more firmly against the girl's head.

The girl screamed.

"Thr—"

The Henry jerked against Hawk's shoulder. A quarter-sized hole appeared in the glass of the door's upper panel. The outlaw stood in the street, now facing the opposite direction from Hawk. He and the girl stood stock-still. For a second, Hawk thought he'd missed his shot.

But then the Stanley rider's arm dropped. He triggered his pistol into the dirt in front of him and the girl. The pistol fell into the dust.

The girl screamed.

The Stanley rider took one stumbling step forward before his legs buckled. He dropped to his knees in the street and then fell forward without trying to break his fall. He lay belly down, kissing the dirt from which he'd come and to which he had so unceremoniously and quickly returned.

The girl staggered away from the dead man, screeching.

Hawk opened the door and stepped out onto the shop's front boardwalk. He looked around, planting the smoking Henry's rear stock to his right hip. Joe Pevney ran out from behind the rain barrel, glanced at Hawk, and then made a beeline to the howling blonde, who kept screaming horrifically as she stared down at the man who'd abducted her.

As Pevney drew the girl to him, hugging her, cooing to her, calming her, Hawk stepped into the street. He scowled at Pevney as the girl sobbed in the barman's arms. He looked at the dead men lying strewn around him, then back to Pevney.

Exasperation burned through the rogue lawman. He'd been prepared to die. His wife and son were waiting for him. But in the same way he'd saved Arliss Coates from the frigid mountain lake, he'd been saved from Stanley's men by Pevney and Whitehall, who'd been emboldened by what they'd perceived as Hawk's own bravery but which had, in fact, been merely a private wish to die.

"Shit," he said now, out loud, as he looked at the dozen men lying twisted and bloody around him.

He couldn't help seeing the irony in the situation, however. A laugh raked up out of his chest. Then another. Then he was walking around, directionless, laughing as though at the funniest joke he'd ever heard.

He saw the doctor walking across the street from his office to where Whitehall sat on the boardwalk beyond Pevney and the still-sobbing girl. The sawbones and Whitehall, as well as the barman and the girl, now stared curiously, apprehensively at the rogue lawman stumbling around in the street near the strewn bodies, guffawing, occasionally tipping his head back to send his bizarre laughter at the blue, sunlit sky.

After a time, Hawk's laughter dwindled to chuckles, which, in turn, dwindled to silence.

The humor was gone.

Now he just felt hollowed out and beaten down.

Hawk sighed, poking his hat brim back off his forehead with his Henry's barrel. He spat into the street and stood, pondering, with a fist on his hip, the Henry resting on his shoulder. Apparently, today hadn't been his day to leave this dung-heap world. And since he had one last loose end to tie up here in Cedar Bend before moving on to his cabin in the mountains, he might as well get to the tying.

He walked over to the livery barn, and saddled his grullo.

He rode to the hotel and loaded his gear onto his horse. Mounting up, he drew his hat brim down over his eyes and galloped west.

Joe Pevney was helping the doctor get Chester Whitehall across the street to his office. A few people were filtering back onto the street after the shooting. A working girl from one of the brothels had taken young Janey Ryan under her wing, and was pouring the understandably distraught child a brandy in the whore's parlor house. The undertakers—both McCauleys—had already pulled their wagon into the street and were busily loading up the bodies, the elder McCauley whistling as he worked.

Pevney stared beyond the undertakers toward Hawk, whose broad-shouldered figure dwindled quickly as he rode out of town, toward the mountains looming beyond.

"What in the hell do you suppose is the matter with him?" the barman asked Whitehall.

"Who knows?" Whitehall said through a pained grunt. "Some people are just naturally colicky, I reckon."

CHAPTER 15

HAWK HAD NO TROUBLE BACKTRACKING THE NOW-dead Stanley men to the Circle S headquarters. There were few well-traveled trails in the mountains, and the dozen riders had left plenty of fresh sign.

As he rode into the high-mountain clearing in which the headquarters was located, he stopped just beyond the wooden ranch portal and looked around. It was high noon, and the headquarters buildings looked washed out and surreal in the harsh, high-altitude sun. The bunkhouse and other outbuildings sat at the base of a rise from the main house, which was impressive.

At least, it had been impressive once.

Now it looked as though it had been abandoned five or six years ago. The rest of the place looked similarly neglected despite the stamp of horse hooves indicating men had lived and worked here. An eerie silence hung heavy. It was relieved by only the whispering breeze and the twittering of birds in the pines surrounding the place.

Hawk touched spurs to the grullo's flanks and rode under the wooden ranch portal bearing the Stanley brand burned into the overhead crossbar, and into the yard.

He glanced around warily, his Henry resting across his saddlebow, as he crossed a corner of the yard and started up the trail climbing the hill to the main house. As he rode, he studied the house carefully. It was awash in brassy sunlight, but the windows resembled the dark, empty eye sockets in a dead man's skull.

Hawk followed the trail's curve up into the driveway, and stopped in front of the shabby picket fence surrounding a yard that had become overgrown before all the transplanted trees, shrubs, and vines had died and turned brown.

The loud banging of a piano assailed Hawk's ears from inside the house. The boisterous clanging had started so abruptly that Hawk's heart quickened, and his fingertips tingled as he tightened his right hand around his Henry's neck.

A man's raspy, off-key voice began singing loudly in accompaniment of the piano's harangue:

> "On the banks of the Roses,
> My love and I sat down,
> And I took out my violin
> To play my love a tune,
> In the middle of the tune,
> Oh, she sighed and she said,
> O-ro, Johnny, lovely Johnny,
> Would you leave me?"

Hawk racked a cartridge into the Henry's action and off-cocked the hammer. Again, his gaze swept the sunlit house. The singing—if you could call it singing and not some mad hybrid of a wail and a howl—continued as he swung down from the grullo's back, dropped the reins in the dust, and pushed through the trellis cluttered with dead vines.

The wailing grew louder as Hawk approached the house via the chipped and cracked stone walk, the broad, once-grand veranda widening before him.

> *"Oh, when I was a young man*
> *I heard my father say,*
> *That he'd rather see me dead*
> *And buried in the clay,*
> *Sooner than be married*
> *To any runaway,*
> *By the lovely sweet Banks of the Roses."*

Extending his Henry from his right hip, his gloved thumb on the hammer, Hawk walked up wooden steps badly in need of fresh paint. He glanced cautiously through the door, which had been propped half-open with a brick. Beyond lay a broad foyer in thick shadow. Dead leaves and dirt littered the wooden floor. Sour air pushed against Hawk as his gaze probed the shadows.

He looked up the stairs that ran up the foyer's right wall.

> *"Oh, then I am no runaway*

And soon I'll let them know,
I can take a good glass
Or can leave it alone;
And the man that does not like me
He can keep his daughter at home
And young Johnny will go roving with
another."

Seeing no one, no movement, Hawk clicked the Henry's hammer back to full cock, and walked into the house. A tall, thick shadow slid out of the darkness behind the stairs. A gun flashed and thundered. The bullet plowed into Hawk's lower right side. He winced as he squeezed his Henry's trigger.

The two reports were like near-simultaneous thunder.

Hawk stumbled backward and hit the floor near the door's threshold. The man-shaped silhouette before him staggered back into the shadows beyond the staircase. Hawk heard a man grunt. The rogue lawman quickly pumped another cartridge into the Henry's action, and fired.

The man-shaped shadow jerked violently backward and fell with a thundering boom as the big man hit the floor.

"And if ever I get married
'Twill be in the month of May—"

The singing as well as the piano-banging stopped abruptly.

Hawk's right side burned. He placed his left hand over the hole. It came away bloody. Grunting, he gained his feet, staggering a little, trying to suppress the pain of the wound. Gritting his teeth, he loudly racked a round into the Henry's chamber.

The piano-banging and singing resumed:

> *"When the leaves they are green*
> *And the meadows they are gay..."*

Hawk followed the wailing and wild piano-hammering through a broken French door and into a large parlor filled with the cloying odor of death. On the parlor's far side, a man with a tumbleweed of curly gray hair growing atop his lean and weathered head banged away at a grand piano on which a man lay belly up, atop what appeared a Confederate flag.

Hawk recognized the stiff figure of Johnny Stanley glaring at the ceiling, knees and boots dangling down the piano's near side.

The old piano player's eyes met Hawk's as he sang:

> *"And I and my true love*
> *Can sit and sport and play*
> *On the lovely sweet Banks of the Roses."*

The man raised his hands from the keys. He stopped singing.

The piano's reverberations dwindled slowly, echoing around the cave-like room.

The man who could only be Mortimer Stanley

lifted a bottle to his lips, and took a long drink. He set the bottle down on the piano, smacked his lips, and stared across the room at Hawk, standing just inside the French doors, aiming the Henry at Stanley from his right hip.

"Do you mean to tell me that you have now killed every one of my men, Mister Hawk?"

Hawk wrinkled his nose with dismay. "I had help."

"Help?" Stanley was incredulous, insulted. He wrinkled his brows angrily. "Who helped you?"

"A couple townsmen couldn't mind their own business."

Hawk moved into the room, sort of dragging his right foot to ease the pressure in that side. Blood dribbled from the wound, over his cartridge belt, and down his right leg. He tossed his rifle onto a leather sofa and walked over to a liquor cabinet between the big fireplace and the piano. He glanced over at Stanley, one brow arched inquisitively.

"Help yourself," the rancher said, flaring a nostril. "I reckon you deserve it."

Hawk lifted a cut glass decanter to his nose, sniffing. He splashed the brandy into a goblet and threw back half. When he'd refilled the glass, he turned to Stanley, wincing with the pain surging through his side and causing his shoulder blades to draw together.

Stanley gave a smile, showing large yellow teeth. "Red Wolf get you?"

"Is that the big man in the foyer?"

Stanley nodded. "He dead?"

"Probably."

Stanley pursed his lips. "You clean up right well, Mister Hawk. But the joke's on you, as well. If you don't get to a sawbones, you're gonna bleed to death." He smiled again, shrewdly. "There ain't no sawbones up here, and I'll be damned if I'll fetch you one."

"That's all right." Hawk grabbed the decanter off the liquor cabinet and, holding the goblet in his other hand, shuffled back over to the sofa. He gave his back to it and sagged gently into it, wincing. "I'll be comfortable right here. Your brandy will kill the pain till it doesn't need killin' anymore."

Stanley looked over his dead son at Hawk, frowning. "Ain't you gonna kill me? Ain't that what you come here for?"

"No." Hawk finished off the brandy in his goblet and awkwardly splashed more into it, slopping some over the side of the glass and onto the sofa. "And yes."

"Explain yourself, sir!" Stanley barked.

Hawk hiked his left shoulder. "I rode out here to kill you, yes." He smiled as he raised the glass to his mouth. "But I've had a change of heart. I'm not going to kill you."

He sipped the brandy, enjoying the soothing burn that washed down inside him, slightly tempering the pain of the bullet wound.

Stanley seemed indignant. "Why not? I tried to kill you. Several times!"

"You're doin' too good a job yourself," Hawk said, and took another, bigger sip of the brandy. He sighed and rested the glass on his right leg. He looked at his wound. Blood continued to flow out of him.

Stanley grabbed the bottle off the piano and rose uncertainly to his feet. He tripped over a leg of the bench as he walked out from behind the piano and turned toward Hawk.

He wore a ratty plaid robe over filthy balbriggans. A pistol hung low on his left leg, on the outside of his robe. His cadaverous cheeks were carpeted in beard stubble the color of metal filings. He stopped and glanced at his son lying dead on the piano to his left. The body was bloating, the cheeks puffing, as though with a held breath.

Stanley glowered at Hawk. "You killed my only boy."

Hawk shook his head. "I only shot him. You killed him a long time ago... when you killed your wife and her lover. Maybe your daughter still has a chance. She left here. She's gonna start a new life for herself... far away from here. Far away from you, Stanley, you sick bastard."

Tears dribbled down the old rancher's cheeks. "You killed him. You killed my boy." He drew the big Colt revolver from the holster on his leg, and clicked the hammer back. He glanced at Johnny once more. "My boy, my boy..."

He jerked his head to Hawk, gritting his teeth, tears continuing to roll down his slack, pasty face. "I'll kill you for that!"

Hawk smiled, raising his drink in one hand. "Don't blame you one damn bit."

Stanley lifted the Colt, aiming down the barrel at Hawk's face.

A gun barked.

Hawk jerked with a start.

He frowned as he stared at Stanley's revolver. There had been no lapping flash of flames from the barrel.

The gun quivered in Stanley's shaky hand. Then the old man's hand opened, and the gun thumped onto the carpeted floor. Stanley staggered backward, eyes wide. He looked down at the hole in his chest from which blood bubbled with each tick of his heart.

Footsteps sounded behind Hawk. A familiar female voice said calmly behind him, "You're right, Gideon. I still have a chance. But when I got to the first relay station, I decided that my chance was here... at home. So I rented a horse from the station manager and rode back here to kill you, Father."

She walked up to the sofa, on Hawk's right side. She glanced at Hawk and then at her father, who had stumbled against the piano. She held an old Remington revolver in her right fist. Smoke curled from the barrel.

"I rode back here to kill you and take over, Father. This ranch hasn't been run right in years. But it's going to be run right now... with you dead... and me in charge. I know this ranch like the back of my hand. I can run it the way a ranch needs to be run."

Slumped backward against his dead son, Stanley stared in exasperation at his daughter. Arliss smiled at him. "Goodbye, Father. Say hello to the devil for me."

Stanley raised his left hand in supplication.

Arliss's pistol popped once, twice. The thunder

blasted off the walls. Stanley jerked as each bullet hammered into him. He grunted and gurgled and rolled off the side of the piano to pile up on the floor.

Arliss stared at him for a moment, looking a little shocked herself.

Then she turned quickly to Hawk, set the smoking pistol down on the floor, and knelt beside him.

"Gideon!" she breathed. "Oh, Gid—I thought for sure they'd killed you!"

"They have," Hawk said. "But it's all right." He smiled at her, brushing his fingers gently across her flushed cheek. "It's all right, Arliss. I'm glad you're here, though. I'm glad you came home. A fresh start... here... at home. That's good."

"A fresh start," Arliss said, leaning down to examine his wound. "That's right, a fresh start—for both of us. You're going to help me get this place in shape."

Hawk frowned at her, then shook his head. "I'm finished, Arliss."

"Pshaw!" Arliss said. "That's nothin' but a flesh wound. As soon as I've sewn you up and got the blood stopped, you'll be good as new. Why, in two weeks, I'll have you hammering nails and slinging paint all over this place!"

She draped Hawk's right arm around her neck and, grunting, hoisted him to his feet.

"Let's get you upstairs. Then I'll fetch some hot water and get to work on that hole."

As Arliss helped him up the stairs, Hawk laughed.

He laughed lest he should cry.

RIDE ALONG WITH A TRUE WESTERN HERO!

If the cash was cold and the trail was hot, bounty hunter
Lou Prophet would run his quarry to the ground. He loved
his work – it kept him in wine and women, and was never,
ever dull. And his latest job sounds particularly attractive.

Her name is Lola Diamond. She is a showgirl, and a prime
witness in a murder trial that's going on without her.
Prophet is supposed to find and "escort" her to the
courthouse, whether she likes it or not. But some very
dangerous men are moving to make sure the pair never
reaches the courthouse alive.

"A storyteller who knows the West."—**Bill Brooks**

AVAILABLE JULY 2022

Peter Brandvold grew up in the great state of North Dakota in the 1960's and '70s, when television westerns were as popular as shows about hoarders and shark tanks are now, and western paperbacks were as popular as *Game of Thrones*.

Brandvold watched every western series on television at the time. He grew up riding horses and herding cows on the farms of his grandfather and many friends who owned livestock.

Brandvold's imagination has always lived and will always live in the West. He is the author of over a hundred lightning-fast action westerns under his own name and his pen name, Frank Leslie.

Manufactured by Amazon.ca
Bolton, ON

25448375R00104